THE CAPTAIN'S CURSE

The river packet was stranded in the storm-swept night like the ark on Mount Ararat, the flood waters swirling around it. On shore, the helpless rescuers watched—incapable of crossing the raging flood to save the passengers.

The captain stood on the boiler deck, screaming curses. "If we die, you too will die. One by one, you'll die; and when you do, the packet will ring its bell and blow its whistle to celebrate the death."

That was years before, but the captain's curse was fulfilling itself. One by one, people did die —some old, some young—and they had this in common: nobody knew what killed them. They just grew weak and . . . died!

Could one eighteen-year-old girl, whose father was now stricken with the cursed disease, hope to solve the terrible mystery and save her father's life?

WHISTLE IN THE WIND
is an original POCKET BOOK edition.

Books by Dorothy Daniels

Blackthorn
Child of Darkness
The Exorcism of Jenny Slade
Ghost Song
The Guardian of Willow House
Illusion at Haven's Edge
The Possessed
The Two Worlds of Peggy Scott
The Unlamented
Whistle in the Wind

Published by POCKET BOOKS

Whistle
in the Wind

Dorothy Daniels

PUBLISHED BY POCKET BOOKS NEW YORK

WHISTLE IN THE WIND

POCKET BOOK edition published January, 1976

L

This original POCKET BOOK edition is printed from brand-new plates made from newly set, clear, easy-to-read type. POCKET BOOK editions are published by POCKET BOOKS, a division of Simon & Schuster, Inc., 630 Fifth Avenue, New York, N.Y. 10020. Trademarks registered in the United States and other countries.

Whistle
in the Wind

ONE

I was not accustomed to being disappointed, not even in the face of unexpected serious events. Besides, this was one of the most important periods in my eighteen years of life. I'd finished my schooling at the convent and soon after made my debut in society at the French Opera House, where mama and I had a box to ourselves.

It is a measure of a New Orleans girl's popularity in how many young men pay their respects at her first opera appearance, and how many opera glasses are turned her way. I'd had more than a score of young men bowing over my hand and I didn't doubt but that every glass in the theater had been aimed at our box at one time or another. I considered my entry into society to have been a great success. I placed part of this triumph on the gown I wore. It was of white satin with a deep V-shaped neckline, sleeveless, with a full vest and jabot. It had been imported from Paris, fitted to my figure by one of the best stylists in New Orleans and I was rightfully proud of the way I was turned out for that occasion.

Beginning at once, young men would come calling, after first being introduced by mutual friends. They would leave their cards and, if invited back, would come for tea and the little cakes mama made.

For that reason I expressed my disappointment to mama. Selfishly, I know now, but those days were vitally important to me, or so it seemed at the time.

"I shall miss the Royal Ball," I argued. "Don't you wish me to find a suitable beau, mama?"

Mama rarely grew exasperated with me, but this time she never hesitated. "I am speaking of your father, Carolyn. He is ill and he has sent for us."

"I know, but there wasn't any indication he is desperately ill. . . ."

"Carolyn, all we have here we owe to him. This fine house, our servants. All the clothing we wish to buy from New Orleans stores or from Paris and London. Nothing is denied us. We simply have the bill sent to him and we never hear anything more about it. And you will admit he has also treated us very generously in our allowance money."

"He can afford it," I said.

"That's not the point. And you know it."

"Mama, what is the mystery behind papa's refusal to let us live with him on the plantation? For years he's seen us only when he's come to New Orleans, perhaps once or twice a year. To me it's almost like not having a father."

"I don't know what his reasons are, but I know my husband and his reasons are good ones, I warrant."

"But why the mystery? He has this large sugar plantation and his big sugar house. I barely remember it. I remember the plantation house, though, and it seemed enormous to me then. A mansion, to say the least. And he lives there all by himself. There must be something wrong."

"At the moment, Carolyn, there is something very wrong or he would not have sent for us. I don't wish to discuss this any longer. You will pack immediately for a prolonged stay."

"I couldn't come later, by myself?"

"I will not have you traveling alone, and it is a long distance to the plantation. Besides, he asked for both of us." She paused and then brought the edge of her handkerchief delicately to her eyes, which were beginning to brim with tears.

"When he was here last January, he looked so thin and pale. He was ill then, though he denied it. He used to be a strapping man."

I felt like crying too, but not for the same reasons she did. I barely knew my father. I did have faint recollections of his taking me horseback riding, holding me fast to the saddle in front of him while he rode over his arpents of sugar cane and gave orders to the men who worked for him. I recalled the overly sweet odor from the mill presses, but the brown sugar, before it was crystallized into white, was a fine type of candy. They'd been wonderful years, but so few, and it was all so long ago.

Mama and I had been suddenly moved to New Orleans and installed in a new, large and opulent house with a large patio, flower filled and as beautiful as the rest of the house. Then began the few occasions when papa would appear and spend perhaps a week with us, during which time he also conducted much of his business. They were happy days. I never had any desire to go back to the plantation, but I know I used to wish papa wouldn't go away so soon after he arrived.

I went up to my room and called Marie to help me pack. She was in tears, far more than mama or I, at the thought of our leaving.

"Stop it, Marie," I said. "We'll soon be back and you're not losing your position here."

"But in this big house it will be so lonely," she said. "And you will not go to the Royal Ball. Have you thought of that?"

"More often than I like to mention. But my father is sick and we have to go to him. If he gets better quickly, we'll soon be back. Perhaps in time for the ball. Now, you start folding my underthings and be careful of them. I'm going to select the dresses. . . ."

I gave a curt laugh. Dresses on the plantation? Nobody dressed there. Formal dinners, beaux calling, important people coming to visit—none of that existed. I even began to wonder if papa would expect us to keep house for him. I wondered how he'd gotten along all these years of living alone.

It required only two hours to pack and dress for traveling. I heard voices and sounds downstairs and I expected that mama was arranging for the journey. When I came down she was ready, setting her large Gainsborough hat on her tight, wheat-colored curls. Mama was a beautiful woman. I could only pray that at her age I would look as attractive and fashionable. She had selected black for traveling, but I favored lighter colors and my hat was a toque, trimmed with black satin, meant for younger faces and very much in style.

Mama glanced at me and smiled slightly. "You look very attractive, my dear. Now, a carriage is waiting to take us to the dock where we will board the *Silver Blossom* for the journey to the plantation. It is better traveling by riverboat than by the dirty steam trains which do not come within seventy miles of the plantation anyway, and we would then have to travel by stage. There is no worse method of traveling, so I have chosen the river."

"I'm delighted, mama. I love the packets. They are like palaces."

Mama signaled the maids, who promptly carried out our luggage, which filled the carriage to such an extent that we had trouble squeezing in ourselves. The maids, led by Marie's loud wailing, cried and waved as the carriage moved away. I felt like crying too.

The ride to the dock was through the center of the city, and New Orleans in 1885 was a wonderful place to live. It was crowded, busy, colorful. There were smells and sounds that would remain with me as long as I lived. The vendors with their baskets of fruit and vegetables, the chimney sweeps, the peddlers of fish and milk, all crying their wares. Huge drays clattered noisily over the brick-paved streets; delivery wagons moved in and out of the confusion. Stately carriages and coaches sedately made their way, and fast buggies, handled by dashing young men, took advantage of every loophole to make faster progress than anyone else. When we passed the French Opera House, I felt a genuine tug at my emotions because the theater represented so much the way of life I was leaving.

"Anyone would think," mama said, somewhat crossly, "that you were never coming back."

"I must come back, mama. I could never live anywhere else. I wouldn't want to."

"You notice that I did not close up the house or dismiss the servants."

"That is what keeps my hopes up. Do you think papa is very ill?"

"I don't know. His message was brief, but I could tell by the writing there must be something seriously wrong. He used to write in a bold script but this was shaky as an old, old man's. He was never one to alarm those he loved and he told nothing of the nature of his illness. That is like him."

"You have seen so little of him these past years, mama, that I wonder if it is possible you are still in love with him."

Mama's eyes flashed in anger, but only for a moment. She laughed curtly. "You are so young, my dear. I fell in love with your father to such an extent I couldn't stay away from him. The day we married was the grandest day of my life and there will never be another to equal it. I loved him immeasurably every day since I have known him. He sent us away for a reason. When he refused to tell me what it was, I knew that it was only to protect us. And I assure you that he loves us as dearly as I love him. Now that I have put you to rights on the matter, we shall not discuss it again."

"Yes, mama," I said. "I'm sorry if I sounded ungrateful. Really I'm not, but . . . but. . . ."

"I know. The opera, the ball, the beaux, the new gowns, the cotillions. Yes, they are wonderful, Carolyn, but there is more to living than that. Much more, as you will find out as the years go by. We have been fortunate, you and I, to have had all the best things in life handed to us by a man who loves us. I repeat, I do not know the secret of the plantation and I will not ask him a question. I beg of you never to mention this strange arrangement he made that we live apart."

"I'll be most careful," I promised. "I think I love papa too. But how can I be sure when I have not seen him more than a month's time in ten years? He is a stranger to me. I do remember how kind he was when we lived at the plantation. I do not remember much about those days but his kindness and love I do."

"That's fine. Now we've got to find roustabouts to

handle our bags. See if you can find two or three of them. We haven't much time. The packet is due to sail in a few minutes."

I found roustabouts and supervised getting our baggage aboard while mama paid our fares and arranged for the best cabin on this opulent, fantastic boat.

It was like entering another world. A small, rather private one, but the packet lacked for nothing. Its main dining hall ran almost the length of the ship. Overhead were crystal chandeliers with oil burning lamps in profusion. Tables were laid with the finest linen and gleaming silver. The carpet was thick and lush and there were huge mirrors everywhere.

The ladies' salon was equally well furnished and our cabin was surprisingly large, with intricately carved furniture, a comfortable bed, window hangings of fine quality and everything done in pale blue.

I was eager to watch the side-wheeler sail, so while mama engaged in unpacking, I went up to the boiler deck where one could see the wharf best. The first mate was bellowing orders, a bell clanged somewhere and the whistle deafened me as the gangplank was hauled in. The mighty wheel began to turn, the twin feathered stacks belched black smoke and we began to move away from the dock. This was an adventure in my life and despite the fact that our journey was inspired by sadness, I still meant to make the most of it.

I returned to the cabin and finished unpacking. I changed into a day dress and clapped a plain sailor hat on my head. I was eager to go on deck again. Mama shooed me out of the cabin, saying I was more of a hindrance than a help.

I walked sedately and in a very ladylike fashion, I hoped, along the carved archway colonnade of the main cabin. I even dared to pause at the silver water cooler to refresh myself, using one of the cups chained to the cooler. Then I went out on deck and paced slowly along, looking at both sides of the river as we steamed by.

The big wheel was making a great deal of noise so I went farther astern. I passed the grand salon, but it was early and few were taking advantage of its ornate comfort.

I looked in the windows of the men's salon where there was a great deal of drinking and card playing going on.

Then I saw a somewhat grizzled man of about fifty, standing at the after rail, smoking a ferocious-looking stogie that seemed to give off as much smoke as the stacks belching high above us.

"You be the Taylor girl, I reckon," he said as I approached him.

"Why, yes," I said. "I am Carolyn Taylor. How did you know me?"

"Saw you come aboard with your ma. She's still a right good-looking woman."

"If you would care to talk to her, sir. . . ."

"Oh, no," he said. He removed the wide-brimmed white hat he wore and rubbed a hand over his almost perfectly bald pate. "No, thank you kindly, miss. She would ask questions I don't care to answer."

"May I ask who you are, sir?"

"You may, but that don't mean I'll tell you. Take my advice, miss. If you see me when you're with your ma, don't let on we met. I don't want to be asked any questions."

"What is this all about?" I asked. "I think I have a right to know why you insist on being so mysterious."

"You may have the right, but you won't learn anything from me. You're going back to the plantation to see your pa. That right?"

"Yes. He sent us a message that he is ill."

"Then you better pray this packet makes good time and doesn't wind up on a sandbar or get pierced by a snag. You don't have much time." He raised his hat again. "Good afternoon, Miss Taylor."

"But . . . can't you at least explain a little. . . ."

He disregarded me, turned and walked away, never looking back. I leaned weakly against the rail he had abandoned, but only for a moment while I collected my wits. I then hurried back to the cabin.

"I just met a man on deck," I said breathlessly. "He knew who I was and he said he saw us come aboard and you were a mighty good-looking woman."

"He knew who you were?" mama asked. "Did he tell you his name?"

"No. He wasn't very friendly, but he also knew we were going back to the plantation because papa was sick."

"What did he look like?"

"Well, I think he was about fifty years old. Kind of heavy. He had brown eyes and he didn't wear any beard or mustache."

"Was he bald? Could you see that?"

"Yes. He removed his hat most politely and he was very bald."

"Anse Austin," she said promptly. "He has a smaller plantation adjacent to ours. What else did he say? Why didn't he come with you to see me?"

"He said he hoped we wouldn't get snagged or wind up on a sandbar because we didn't have much time."

"Much time for what?" Her face paled a bit. "He means Eric must be very ill."

"I'm sure that's what he meant, mama."

"We're going looking for him. I want to find out exactly what he meant. Anse is in a position to know what's going on. Come along, we'll search for him."

We searched until supper time without finding a trace of him. He didn't appear in the dining room and after we ate, mama weighed the idea of asking the purser which was Anse Austin's cabin.

"It would not be according to the rules of etiquette for a woman to ask the number of a man's cabin, but I'm not going to abide by the rules. Come along."

The purser had closed his office for the night, but when we asked one of the deck hands to fetch him he came willingly enough, a fine-looking man in his blue uniform adorned with brass buttons.

"How may I be of service to you ladies?" he asked.

"There's an old friend of the family aboard," mama explained. "My daughter met him, but I have not had the pleasure and I wish to talk to him. He is Mr. Anse Austin and he has a plantation next to ours."

"I know Mr. Austin. He often travels with us, ma'am, but I can't give you the number of his cabin. I'm sorry."

"But why not? He is an old friend."

"Mr. Austin got off at the last stop."

"But I saw him not two hours ago," I protested.

"No doubt. While you ladies were enjoying supper, we docked briefly and Mr. Austin got off."

"Was he scheduled to leave the packet at that landing?" mama asked.

"No, ma'am. He said something about the fact that he would stay over for the next packet because he wasn't of a mind to tell bad news."

Mama nodded and we turned away. I said, "How long before we reach the plantation, mama?"

"Day after tomorrow, in the morning. Perhaps we should have taken the steam train after all. It might have been a bit faster."

"I wonder why Mr. Austin didn't want to tell us about papa. That's what he must have meant when he spoke to the purser."

"I don't know, my dear, but I'm afraid this is going to be more serious than we feared. Mr. Austin has always been an honest and outspoken man."

"He did seem that way to me," I said. "But why in the world didn't he have the courage to tell us what ails papa? He didn't seem like a man afraid to tell bad news."

"I don't know why he left the ship to avoid seeing me, but the fact that he did is the cause of much worry, Carolyn. I shall be most impatient for the rest of the journey so please forgive me if I'm curt and perhaps short-tempered with you. I wish to return to our cabin now. I was thoughtful enough to have provided myself with sleeping draughts and tonight I intend to take one."

TWO

On the morning of the second day, the packet drew up to the pier and papa's plantation. From this dock most of his sacks of sugar and barrels of syrup were sent off to market. I had vivid memories of a place constantly piled high with the products of his plantation, with roustabouts and plantation hands busily moving about between the towering rows of barrels and sacks.

We found the dock completely empty. There wasn't a thing on it and not a soul appeared. I'd never seen such utter desolation. Mama realized it too and spoke to the packet captain before we disembarked.

"Yes, ma'am," he said, "ain't been much shipping out of here lately. Can't remember the last time we picked up cargo, or were even signaled there was a passenger. Kinda thought the plantation had just gone out of business."

"I don't understand it," mama said. "It has been my belief my husband was very busy and successful."

"Can't say as to that, ma'am. All I know is there's never any cargo. Now, shouldn't there be someone to meet you folks?"

"I suppose so," mama said. "My husband doesn't know exactly when we're due to arrive, but he knew it would be soon."

I said, "I don't like the looks of this, mama. Something must be wrong."

"Ma'am," our captain suggested, "maybe if I blow the whistle some there'll be a carriage sent."

16

"Thank you, Captain," mama said gratefully. "I would be obliged."

In a few minutes the packet whistle sounded four times, its deep notes seeming to echo for miles around. Our baggage was now ashore and we waited hopefully while the packet slowly moved away from the dock with more hooting of its whistle. Perhaps ten or fifteen minutes went by. The packet was disappearing upriver and mama and I stood beside the mound of baggage wondering just what we ought to do. There were no houses, not even cabins nearby and nowhere to seek help.

"Your father should have sent someone to meet every boat," mama complained. "There are not so many of them to keep him busy all day waiting for us."

"Doesn't he have a great number of people working for him?" I asked. "He certainly could have sent someone."

"I'm afraid, Carolyn, that we must be patient. I do not care to walk and leave all this baggage behind. Besides, it's a long way to the plantation."

I was about to add a few comments of my own when we saw a cloud of dust far down the road and presently a carriage appeared, driven by someone who was urging the horse to its best speed.

Mama said, "I do hope he is coming for us, but I declare I don't recognize the man."

As he pulled up I could see that he was young, a year or two older than I, perhaps. He was tall too, enough that he seemed awkward in getting down off the carriage. He was in working clothes, wore no hat and he was most apologetic as he reached us.

"Ma'am, miss, I got here as fast as I could when we heard the whistle. My pa told me to be on the lookout for you when any packet pulled in, but I got busy with the morning chores and I didn't realize a packet was here until I heard the whistle."

"At any rate," mama said, "you are here and we're very pleased that you are. May I ask who you are, sir?"

"I'm not very bright, I guess," he said with an abashed grin. "I'm Randolph Austin. Anse's son. You know, we've got the next plantation."

"Of course," mama said. "You've grown so I didn't recognize you. This is Carolyn. You may remember her."

"It was years ago, mama," I remonstrated.

"I remember you," he said with a smile. "You were the prettiest girl I ever saw, then or since. I remember all right."

"We met your father on the boat," mama said. "He got off at the first landing so we didn't get to talk to him. He and Carolyn had a few words, that was all."

"Why'd he do that? Get off the boat? He was coming straight home, far as I knew."

"I don't know, Randy," mama said. "How are things on our plantation?"

"And why didn't my father come to meet us?" I added.

"Couldn't. He's too sick. He asked us to be on the lookout. He said you were due very soon, but you got here faster'n I thought you would."

"Do you know what ails my husband?" mama asked.

"No, ma'am. What ails lots of others around here, I guess. You better get into the carriage and we'll have to crowd onto the front seat so I can get some of this baggage in back. I'll return for what I can't load. No call to worry about it. Nobody comes here and it'll be safe."

We obediently climbed onto the carriage. Randy busied himself with the luggage and mama looked extremely worried.

"I'm very concerned," she said. "There's something wrong here. I wish that young man would hurry."

"Mama, I'm going to ask him some questions. We ought to be prepared for what we may find."

"Yes, that's a good idea. He made it seem that others are also sick, or have been. Your father should have written and told me what is wrong. I'm glad we didn't delay."

Randy squeezed about half the luggage into the carriage before he got aboard and we began the jouncing trip to the plantation some three miles away. That is, the house was three miles from the dock. Papa owned all this land, clear to the riverfront and for some miles on either side of the dock. It was one of the largest plantations in this part of Louisiana.

"Hasn't the doctor told anyone what's wrong with my father?" I asked.

"I don't think he knows," Randy replied. "He sure didn't with the others."

"What do you mean, the others?"

"Well, lots of folks around here died during the last few years. That's all I can say. We don't know much about it."

"Without any reason for their deaths?"

"Some . . . oh sure. Some, we all knew what they died of. But there were others. . . ."

"You're not telling us everything we should know," I accused. "Is my father going to die?"

"Can't say. Doc Shea says he's been some better lately."

I didn't know what else to ask so I was silent for a time. The carriage made a slow curve in the dirt road and we seemed to be atop a low plateau looking down over the more fertile acres of the plantation. Soon now the mansion would come into view, if my memory served me well.

Then I saw it! For a few seconds I didn't know what it was, but I quickly remembered. At the very top of a knoll, starkly outlined against the morning sky, were the skeletal remains of a once garish and well-known riverboat. The *Roger Clinton* had been, in its day, one of the most luxurious.

"Is that thing still there?" I asked.

"You mean the *Roger Clinton?*" Randy said, without looking at me. "Yep, figure it'll be there when the world ends."

"Why doesn't someone get rid of it? Why does papa tolerate it there?"

"Nobody wants to take the risk, Miss Carolyn. Been there for eighteen years now. You look at it close you'll see it hasn't busted up any."

"It just stands there," mama said, "like the ark on Mount Ararat. But there's something sinister about that old burned-out hulk of a packet. Maybe I have that impression because I remember when it ran aground."

We were closer to the hulk now. Most of it was blackened from the fire but the parts untouched by smoke or flames seemed as brightly painted as when the packet was new. Its two feathered stacks appeared to have withstood the passage of time well and they looked as if smoke could come belching out at any time.

I had never been permitted to investigate the wreck. In fact, papa ordered me, in his firmest voice, not to go near it. I'd wondered why then, and I still did.

Mama said, "Do you recall when the packet was wrecked, Randy?"

"No, ma'am. I guess I was asleep that night. I wasn't more'n a baby anyhow. I heard what happened, but there are so many stories I don't know which one to believe."

"I know the true one," mama said.

"Tell me," I implored.

"Not now. It's an ugly story, not one I'm proud of. Nor is anyone else, I well imagine. We're going to be at the house in a few more minutes. I'm too worried about your father to do any explaining now."

"I'll remind you," I said.

Randy gave a loud laugh. "No need to," he said. "You'll hear it, all right. From the few people left on your plantation, and from everybody in the village. They still talk about it like it happened yesterday."

I lost interest in the old hulk too, for we had come into sight of the house. It was a mansion. Within those walls were more than sixteen rooms, all of them large, even to servants' quarters on the top floor. Seven great Tuscan columns formed a single colonnade along the facade. The windows were deep set and, like the front door, arched. It was painted white and it seemed to sparkle in the morning light. The green blinds provided a pleasing contrast. There was a row of elephant ear plants, looking forlorn and uncared for.

The formal gardens were in bloom, though somewhat bedraggled, for lack of attention had taken its toll. The cypress and oaks were decorated with so much moss they were showing the effects of the strangling influence of the growth.

To me it looked both cheerful and forlorn, though how

it could possibly be both was far beyond me. I knew what it looked like inside, unless that too had been allowed to deteriorate. The rooms were all in pastels. Mama had insisted on it so the place would be as cheerful as color could make it. She'd been expert and careful in the selection of the furniture and that, too, reflected the gayness of her nature and her desire for color and more color.

The carriage pulled up and we promptly got out to hurry to the entrance. The door opened before we reached it and I hoped to see papa come rushing out with a warm greeting. Instead a tall, black-haired, angular woman in a long brown dress, bowed her head as we approached. She was, I judged, a Jamaican. Middle-aged, but she must have been lovely in her younger days for she was most eye catching now.

"*Bonjour, madame. Bonjour, mademoiselle.* I am Yvonne Cardelay, your husband's housekeeper."

"Good morning," mama said, somewhat taken aback. It was clear she had no knowledge papa had employed a housekeeper. "I pray that you are well."

"*Très bien, merci.*" She turned to English which she spoke well, though somewhat accented. "I wish I could say the same for Monsieur Taylor. He is one sick man."

"I shall go to him at once. Carolyn, see to the luggage and thank the young man for helping us. Please come upstairs as soon as you can."

I merely asked Randy to place the luggage in the reception hall, which was large and ran the whole length of the house, with a curved mahogany staircase which mama was ascending as fast as she could, followed more sedately by Yvonne.

"Thank you very much," I told Randy. "I hope we will see you again soon."

He grinned amiably. "Wouldn't be surprised, seeing I'll be back with the rest of your luggage in about an hour or so. No need to thank me, Miss Carolyn. It's been a real pleasure."

I ran up the stairs without looking into any of the rooms. On the second floor I saw an open door and heard voices. I hurried into the room, edging around Yvonne who all but blocked the doorway. Mama was embracing papa and trying hard not to cry.

Papa was propped up on a mound of pillows, his skin as white as the bed linen. He seemed almost skeletal to me. A man half-dead and half-alive. I restrained my tears. It wasn't easy, for he was pathetic looking and even more so in his gratitude for our coming back. I kissed him on the cheek and held his other hand. Mama was slowly caressing his wrist and forearm as she spoke.

"Eric, you should have let us know things were so difficult here. We had no idea or we'd have come much sooner."

"I wanted Carolyn to have her debut," he said in a voice which, from the way he appeared, should have been weak and tremulous, but was as strong as ever. "It's important to a girl. Especially a very pretty one."

"Papa," I chided him gently, "what is a debut at the opera house compared to caring for someone you love? I'm ashamed of myself for not coming sooner. Though, how could we have known?"

"It's my fault. I kept putting it off." He looked over my shoulder. "Yvonne, please bring chairs for my wife and my daughter."

"*Oui*," Yvonne said and dragged two heavy chairs over, placing them on either side of the bed. It was a relief to sit down. I was suddenly very weary, but at least some of the worry had left me because I knew papa was still alive and with mama's help I thought we could bring him back to sound health.

Now that we were here and more or less settled, I took time to look about the room. So far as I could remember, little had changed. In the rest of the house mama had insisted on being the judge of what was best, but in this room, which she once shared with papa, she had let him have his way. Therefore, unlike the rest of the rooms, this bedroom was done in heavy wood paneling which made it too dark, a burgundy carpet which added no lightness, drapes to match and a fireplace of ebony. Had the furniture been rendered in light tones, the somberness of the room itself might have been relieved, but papa liked dark wood for the dresser, the chiffonier, the two bureaus and even the occasional tables. To me it bore a stronger resemblance to a mortician's parlor than it did a modern 1885 bedchamber in a great and wonderful house.

Mama said, "First of all, my dear, I want to know the nature of your illness. And whether or not you approve of the doctor."

"The doctor is young. Boyd Shea is his name, as I think I wrote you some time back. He came here about ten years ago, just before you . . . went to the city. He's capable and I regard him as a fine physician. Of course, being the only one, this might influence me to some extent. I'm joking of course. Everyone here likes and trusts him."

"I'm pleased to know that. Now, what is wrong with you, Eric?"

"He doesn't know and neither do I. It's a wasting kind of illness. There's no pain, just a weakness that seems to keep growing. I had to give up field work some time ago."

"Did this come upon you suddenly?" mama inquired.

"Very slowly, without any awareness, until the sickness had such a foothold I couldn't shake it off. I've discovered the best medicine is complete rest, so I spend most of my time in bed."

"Who then cares for the plantation and the sugar house?"

"Calvin Lindsay. He's been my overseer for years. It's not his fault things are not going well."

"I gathered that from the lack of shipping that showed on the landing. What's wrong?"

Papa sighed and shook his head. "Lack of help."

"But why should that be? There were always plenty of men willing to work hard for a dollar."

"They're still here, but they don't want to work on our plantation."

"Why not?" mama asked bluntly.

"Now comes the explanation I've dreaded," papa said. "I don't know how to tell you this because I don't believe it myself. You must first understand that we live close to Cajun country and there is a great deal of superstition prevailing. I'm a hardheaded businessman and farmer and

I spent the first years of my life in the North. So I find it hard to reconcile myself to these superstitions. But they exist, and they seem to have a good foothold on the plantation."

"Well, I certainly want more of an explanation than that," mama said.

"Are you trying to tell us this house is haunted?" I asked. I noticed, before papa replied, that Yvonne had silently withdrawn, though the bedroom door had been left wide open.

"Ghosts?" he said. "I'm not sure. I have to tell it. This began years ago when the packet got stuck and burned. No doubt you recall that night, Leah?"

Mama nodded. "How well. I can still hear them screaming."

"Then for Carolyn's benefit let me relate how it all happened. That night there was a severe rainstorm, almost a hurricane. It had been raining for days . . . sometimes it had seemed for weeks. The packet was proceeding downstream with the river current—a badly swollen river too— behind it and making remarkable speed. Suddenly there was a crevasse. The river left its banks, opening a wide channel into which the packet sailed at high speed. It was impossible to slow down or stop the ship, or even maneuver it. The packet came out of the river with bells ringing and whistle sounding until everyone around was awakened by the racket."

"I doubt many slept because of the storm," mama added.

"The packet ran aground right where it stands now. It caught fire when the furnace got too hot and two of the boilers blew up. Mind now, it was raining terribly hard, the water was twelve feet high all around the packet and more water kept pouring in from the break in the river bank. Some of us tried to reach the packet, but it was impossible. I sent all the men I could find down to the pier to carry back any kind of a small boat they could find. There was none. The river had risen there and all the small boats had broken free and were either crushed or taken downstream by the current."

"And nobody could get off the packet?" I asked in horror. "I never knew that before."

"It wasn't the type of story to tell to a little girl," mama said. "Go on, Eric."

"So we stood watching helplessly. Some passengers jumped into the water and were quickly drowned. The captain stood on the boiler deck screaming curses on the people he could see and who would not come to his aid. We were carrying torches, so we were not hiding. The plain fact, which the captain would not, or could not, recognize, was that nobody could reach the packet. He kept shouting that if they all died, we too would die. One by one we'd die over the years, and every time one of us did die, the packet would ring its bell and blow its whistle to celebrate the death."

"Eric," mama said in alarm, "it never really happened? The bells and the whistle and . . . the deaths?"

"It is the reason why I insisted you and Carolyn leave the plantation. That was ten years ago, right after it all began. But it did happen. I wanted my family safe from this awful thing."

"How many have died?" I asked in horror.

"Fourteen, so far. Some old, some young, but they had one thing in common: nobody knows what killed them. They just . . . died."

"And the bell rang and the whistle blew as the packet captain had threatened?" I asked.

"Yes," papa told us. "In every case."

THREE

Papa grew tired after relating that part of his story, so mama closed the blinds and the door and left him alone to sleep and rest. Now we had an opportunity to look over the rest of the house. There was a cook in the kitchen who was quitting at the end of the week, even though she did not live in and her husband drove her to and from work each day. The two nervous and unpredictable maids reported at seven in the morning and went home at eight in the evening. No servant slept in except Yvonne.

I had always loved the big ballroom with its four chandeliers and two fireplaces. Here mama's influence was to be seen in bright carpets and light wood furniture. The color of the walls was somewhere between a blue and a green and it brightened that part of the house tremendously. The furniture, unlike most living rooms at this time of the century, wasn't crowded in. There was a great deal of it, however, but in a space sufficient to accommodate it. The wall were literally papered with paintings, they were hung that close together. Some of the work was valuable, I realized as I studied them more carefully.

There was a large and well-equipped business office on the first floor also, reached from the reception hall and from the back of the house. Here were papa's ledger books, his files, his large teakwood desk and the high-backed chair behind it. The room should have been called a library, for the walls were all lined with bookcases.

The dining room was ample enough to seat better than a score of guests. The long oak table, the matching serving tables and the big buffet were highly polished to bring out the beauty of the wood. It was a lovely room.

My bed chamber was done in a medium blue and mama's in pink. The furniture was rather simple in design. My bed, a half tester, was in white with fine gold lines and no decoration other than that. The pedestal dressing table was oversized and had a large looking glass atop it. There was another full-sized looking glass installed in the center door of the wardrobe. Four soft-cushioned chairs were done in a pale color to match the walls. I'd grown up in this room and I loved it.

We had skipped dinner at noon and by suppertime we were famished. Most of the day, after papa awakened again, was taken up with brief visits to his bedside, and with unpacking. It wasn't until after supper that mama and I had time for serious talk. This began as mama complimented Yvonne on how well the house had been cared for.

That she was pleased was quite obvious. *"Merci, madame.* I do my best."

"You've been here how long now?" I asked.

"Since a few weeks after you and your mama left for New Orleans."

"All that time," I said, "and papa never let mama know. Don't you think that strange, Yvonne?"

"No indeed, *mademoiselle.* It was his wish that you know little about the plantation, for he feared you would wish to come back and that would have been impossible."

"Yvonne, there's no need to stand there. Please sit down. Certainly we must regard you as one of the family after those years of such faithful service."

"It has been my pleasure," she said, and she sat down in the most graceful way I have ever seen a woman seat herself. "Some of the days were good, Most were not. There were the deaths."

"Tell us about some of them," mama said.

"It was a powerful curse. It has lasted all these years. As I understand it, the captain cast that curse upon all those who stood by and let the ship burn and the passengers and crew die. It was impossible to reach them, but the captain, standing there on the deck, didn't know that. All he could see were people who might help and who did not."

"Those who died were really among the people who were gathered to watch the packet burn?" I asked.

"*Oui,* that is so. As more and more of them died, all of us grew more frightened. Sometimes I think the deaths were not as bad as the sound of the whistle and the ringing of the bell. For they sounded just before, or right after the death happened. It is an evil and terrifying thing to hear those sounds and know they tell us someone has just died."

"Didn't anyone ever go aboard and investigate?" I asked.

"Many, many times, until the last two or three years. All of us were too frightened to go aboard. We thought perhaps that it had a bad effect on us."

I wanted to know more about the wreck itself. "The packet seems to stand on top of a hill. How could that have happened?"

Mama answered my question. "The water kept rising, taking the ship with it. When it ran aground it was on top of that knoll. The water receded after it was all over, and returned to its natural banks, where levees were built and have since held. But the packet remained on top of the knoll because there was no way to bring it down."

I said, "Tomorrow I'm going to board that old hulk and see for myself that there is nothing to harm anyone. It's all silly to think a curse could kill all those people."

"Yvonne," mama said, "what do you think of the curse?"

"*Madame,* I am from Jamaica where we believe in many things that would seem strange to you. We have believed in curses for centuries, and sometimes we find ways of warding them off, but not this one. I have used every method I know, but they make no difference."

"Who has recently died?" mama asked. "Someone who worked on the plantation?"

"Martin Duprez, *madame.* He was an expert in determining when the sugar was going to crystallize. Since his death it has been impossible to find anyone with his skill, so the sugar house is not being used. What cane is harvested is sent away to become sugar."

"Because there is a lack of help?"

"*Oui*. Few are left and they will not remain long if . . . anything more should happen. . . ."

"I know what you mean. Now, about Martin Duprez's death. What do you know about it?"

"He became ill. Dr. Shea was called and said he could find nothing wrong with him. That was the sign the curse was working. Always there is nothing wrong that the doctor can find. Monsieur Duprez, he grew pale and weak until he could no longer walk. He took to his bed and for three months he lay there, unable to sleep. He had to be fed and toward the end he raved, mostly about being able to see the people jump from the packet and being able to hear the captain yelling his curse upon us. Then he . . . died. And the steamship whistle blew and the bell clanged. It was much like all the others."

"You seem well educated, Yvonne," mama said. "You told that remarkably well."

"*Oui*, it was a good convent that took me in as a child. I did well there. It is my hope that you will let me remain here. I have been very happy to serve *monsieur*."

"I wouldn't think of changing or even doing without you. Tell me, do you really believe in ghosts and hauntings? Do you think there is a ghost aboard the packet, or many ghosts?"

"Something is there, *madame*, otherwise how does the bell ring and the whistle blow so close to the time of a death? I, for one, would never set foot on the deck of that ship. And, *mademoiselle*, I would not advise you to go there."

"I'm going," I said. "Please don't tell papa what I intend to do. It would only worry him."

"And he would give you a strict command not to go there," mama added. "I too do not advise it, but," she glanced at Yvonne, "Carolyn is a headstrong girl who will have her own way."

Yvonne arose just as gracefully as she had seated herself. "Then if you must go there, do not go alone, please."

"All right. That may be wise. Thank you, Yvonne."

She began making the rounds of the house, locking up,

straightening things. Her devotion to the house was complete and even uniquely so. I wondered if this devotion also extended itself toward papa in a personal way. They had been together for many years. I knew mama was worried about the same thing.

At nine, because we were exhausted from the journey and depressed by the news at the plantation, mama and I decided to retire early. I went to my room and stood at one of the tall windows looking out over the front of the estate. I was glad that my room was not on the north side, where I would perhaps have a view of the old wreck. It was not a comforting sight. There was only a half-moon, but its light was strong enough to illuminate the estate and I thought it beautiful, even if it had been neglected. The gardners, mama and I learned, had quit two months ago because of their fear of the ghosts on the packet who gleefully rang a bell and blew the whistle when someone died. I wondered about that whistle. The bell, I knew from my inspection of one during our trip upriver, might last for many years. It was of brass and heavy so its destruction was virtually impossible. The whistle was something else. It too was of metal, but not made of anything heavy and durable. Besides, to blow a whistle required the use of steam and how could steam be gotten up on a deserted wreck?

I was too tired for more thinking, so I prepared for bed. I blew out the bedside lamp finally and settled down to get some rest. When mama and I had looked in on papa just before we went to our rooms, we'd found him cheerful and feeling a bit better. Or so he informed us. I was hoping we could bring him back to sound health after all, and I was looking forward to my talk with Dr. Shea.

I had dropped off quickly and I slept for about three hours, or until a short time after midnight. I was awakened by the sound of a bell. Its meaning didn't come to me as I sleepily sat up, more annoyed than alarmed. Then the sound of the whistle pierced the night silence—a hoarse, low blast. Both it and the bell certainly came from the area where the old hulk sat atop the knoll.

"Papa!" I shouted. "Papa!"

Without pausing to throw on a robe or wear slippers, I raced out of my room, down the hall and found papa's door wide open. Mama was already there. Papa was sitting up, fully awake and looking now worse than he had before we retired.

"It must have been Tom Horton's time," he said weakly. I noted that his hands were tightly clasped, but they had a tendency to shake anyway. "Tom's been sick longer than me."

"Just so long as that whistle wasn't meant for you," mama said.

"Dr. Shea will likely come by soon. He knows how worried I'd be over the sound of that damned whistle."

"I hope he does. I'd like a talk with him," mama said, voicing my sentiments as well. "You do not feel weaker? There isn't any pain now, is there?"

"Never was," papa said. "I'm not any weaker. I'm nervous. I admit that, but who wouldn't be? Poor Tom! Leah, I do not know how much more of this I can stand."

"I know, darling. But you're all right now. This will pass. Tomorrow Carolyn and I are going to find out what's behind it."

"Good heavens, Leah, we know what's behind it. All I want is to learn how to put a stop to it."

"There will be a way," mama said with a confidence I didn't think she possessed. "There's bound to be."

Papa said, "You don't believe that, do you?"

"I'm afraid not, Eric. And I think it was wrong of you to send me and Carolyn away."

"I did it for your own good. So many have died. So very many, Leah. I didn't want you or Carolyn exposed to such danger. Please don't laugh at this. It wouldn't even be well to doubt it because these things have happened over and over. I beg of you, take Carolyn and return to New Orleans."

"I couldn't do that, Eric."

"And I refuse to go back," I said with all the bravado of an eighteen-year-old. "There are no such things as ghosts and curses. I'm not afraid."

"I am," papa said. "I've been too close to this."

"What of the plantation and the sugar house?" mama asked. "Can I do anything to help there?"

Papa shook his head wearily. "We keep going, after a fashion, but we're not lost yet. Besides, even if it fails, it doesn't matter for we have enough to live on, and very well, too."

"Then why not leave here at once?" mama suggested. "In that way you can get clear of this curse, if that's what's responsible for all this tragedy."

"That won't work either. Three families left the village and moved on to the nearest city. They were sick when they left and they hoped to get away from the influence of that curse. It didn't work. They all died. Besides, I will not abandon the plantation. Now, please go to bed, both of you. I'm all right. The whistle wasn't meant for me."

He might as well have added "this time," for he almost said it aloud. I left while mama helped him get settled for sleep, if he could find it. Minutes later she joined me downstairs in the kitchen where I'd begun to boil water for tea. I set out two places and found some little biscuits which I heated in the big range oven.

"Thank you for being so thoughtful," mama said. "I'm afraid there'll be no more sleep for me this night."

"Nor for me. Mama, do you really think it's possible for someone to curse a number of people and have the curse slowly kill them?"

"No, I do not."

"Neither do I, but papa seems to think it's true."

"My dear, your father is very ill. Others were struck down with what seems to be the same illness, though nobody knows what it is. He has seen these others die. Naturally he's frightened. I'd be terrified."

"I'm still going to get aboard the packet if I can. I refuse to believe in these things, mama. Therefore I'm not afraid. Not exactly," I added. "I admit something is going on that is most mystifying."

We discussed the destruction of the packet and the grisly deaths of a hundred and ten passengers and crew members. Mama's recollection of the tragedy was vivid even after all those years and her retelling of it did little to add to my comfort. I tried to sleep, after we had our tea, but it proved impossible until just before dawn. I lay in bed expecting to hear the bell and then the whistle, and wondering how an abandoned, burned-out riverboat could still get up enough steam to make its whistle blow. Clearly I had to get aboard.

I was delayed in the morning with the arrival of Dr. Boyd Shea. He stepped out of his buggy to stand very slim and tall as I approached to greet him. He had sandy-colored hair, mild blue eyes, a strong-looking face and he was undeniably quite handsome. Well dressed too, in a dark-gray, single-breasted, square-cut sack suit. He reached into the buggy and picked up his little black medicine bag.

"Good morning," he said, lifting his hat as he spoke. "You are, of course, Carolyn."

"Good morning, Doctor. Yes, you're right. Will you look at my father right away, please? He was terribly upset last night when the whistle blew and that bell sounded."

"I presumed he would be. I'll have to give him some bad news, but I know he won't be put off. One of his friends died last evening."

"When the whistle sounded, Doctor?"

He nodded. "I see you know the situation. Yes . . . it happened a few minutes before. We've an ugly problem here, Miss Carolyn. I wish I knew how to handle it."

I fell into step as we walked toward the house. "Haven't you any idea what ails my father?"

"All I can say is it's the same thing that's ailed a lot of other people in this village and plantation. They just seem to get sick, finally go to bed and slowly die despite anything I can do."

"Do you believe the curse is responsible?"

He brought me to a stop. "Now, Miss Carolyn, I'm a medical man. You are a well-educated girl. I cannot believe in such things and I doubt you do."

"Very well, I too find that I cannot. However, if this is not the result of some curse, what kills these people? Why is my father bedfast and clearly not improving?"

"I don't know. I find it hard to treat him, just as I discovered with all the others who were afflicted. It's like a small epidemic, confined to this particular area, consisting of the village and the plantation. Not one victim ever responded to whatever I was doing. Or trying to do. I admit that I'm baffled."

"Yet you deny a belief in the curse of a ship's captain?"

"I must. I wouldn't be true to my profession if I did not."

"Yes, I understand," I said. "Would it be of any value to send my father to a hospital?"

He shook his head. "I don't believe he would survive the journey. And I sent two men to a hospital in Baton Rouge. They both died a day or two later. We did an extensive investigation as to the nature of their deaths and we came up with no answers. This is something to try a man's belief in the science he professes."

"I'm sure you do all you can, Doctor. My mother is upstairs with my father. She'll be happy to see you. And would you tell me, later, how you find him?"

"Indeed I will. With considerable pleasure." His somber attitude disappeared for a few seconds. "You're an exceptionally attractive young lady, Miss Carolyn. I shall admit now that when I call to see your father my visit shall have two purposes, one quite selfish."

I smiled my appreciation of the compliment, but I gave him no answer. Instead, I remained in the living room, waiting for him to come down.

Yvonne, armed with a dust cloth, entered the room and made her way to my side, flipping the cloth over each object of furniture she passed. I knew it was only an excuse to talk to me.

"*Bonjour, mademoiselle,*" she said. "I hope that you slept well."

"Not after what happened last night, Yvonne."

"*Oui,* it is tragic. I can assure you nobody in the village or on the plantation slept well. Another poor man gone. I do not know what to make of it."

"I think they are being murdered," I said. "And I think there's more to it than just a curse, even if it was delivered by a man who thought he had cause to curse the whole world."

"Murdered? Perhaps. Who knows? And it will go on until we find a means to stop it."

"If we are to believe in this, is there such a means?" I asked. "Can there be a way to satisfy the soul of a vengeful man so he will stop these deaths?"

"There are incantations, there are *ouangas*. Oh yes, there are ways, but I do not think any will be effective. It will not stop until the last man who refused to try to rescue the passengers and crew is dead."

"If I thought that, Yvonne, I'd bundle my father into a carriage and rush him away from here even if it seemed the trip might kill him, for he would certainly be bound to die here. If the curse is true."

"It is true, *mademoiselle*. I give you my word. It is true."

Her dogged insistence was making me grow angry, but Dr. Shea came down the stairs and saved me from arguing with her. Dr. Shea shrugged his shoulders like a man totally defeated.

"He is no worse, but neither is he any better. This is the way it goes with all of them. Suddenly there is a crisis and they go downhill very fast while I can do nothing but stand around and pray for a miracle."

"Am I to assume, then, that there is no hope for my father?"

"Indeed not, Miss Carolyn. There is always hope. I would find it hard to function as a doctor if I didn't believe that."

"Then," I said with what I hoped passed for a smile, "I have all the confidence in the world in you, sir."

"Thank you. I left medicine. Your mother will see he gets it at the proper time."

"Thank you," I said. He bowed low over my hand and gave me one last admiring glance as he stepped into his buggy. Then he was off in a cloud of dust and I immediately ceased to think about him. I had something important to do. It might also be dangerous. Whichever it turned out to be, I had to dress for it, so I hurried back into the house and up to my room.

FOUR

In a heavy skirt and gray blouse, both old, I thought I could manage aboard the packet, and not completely ruin good clothes. I laced on a pair of high shoes too, with flat heels, so I could get about easily. I carried a scarf which I intended to tie over my head, and I wore gloves to guard against the fifteen years' accumulation of dirt and grime.

I had to provide myself with a horse and some sort of conveyance, for I did not ride. At the stables I encountered a man I dimly remembered because of his size. He was a heavy man, but carried his weight easily on a six-foot three- or four-inch frame. He would be Calvin Lindsay, papa's overseer. He was not dressed in work clothes, but quite handsomely in a blue serge suit, a black tie over a white shirt. Suddenly I realized he was going to attend the rites for the man who died so mysteriously last night.

"I'm sure I remember you, Mr. Lindsay." I offered him my hand. "You don't seem a day older."

It would have been difficult to guess at his age because his face was so tanned and wrinkled from the sun, but he moved about well, so I doubted he was over forty.

"Miss Carolyn. I may not look any different, but you sure changed. You were just a little girl when you went away."

"It's nice to see you again," I said. "I trust you have not been affected by these stories about a curse."

"Maybe not me, but I know a lot of people who have been. I feel nothing yet, beyond what has happened to your father. And to the plantation."

36

"It's a shame. I wish we could do something about it."

"What?" he shrugged. "The men, they come and work and someone dies and the damned whistle blows and off they go. There has been many a batch of syrup ready for crystallization, ruined by their leaving. And then, your papa, so sick. . . ."

"Mr. Lindsay, hasn't anything ever been done to try and find out what goes on at the old hulk? I mean . . . whistles can't blow without steam; bells can't be rung unless someone is there to ring them."

"And that," he said, "is what makes them all the more scared, Miss Carolyn. There never is anybody there. It just . . . happens."

"Bosh," I said. "It can't happen if nobody is there. I intend to find out more and I'm not going to wait until the whistle blows again. Thank you for telling me all this. And thank you also for not leaving papa as so many of the others have done."

I walked away from him only to find that he was following me. I turned about out of curiosity.

"The hostler left two years ago. I take care of the horses now and I suppose it's a horse you're after."

"And a buggy," I said. "It never occurred to me to ask you to harness a buggy for me."

His big, wide face wreathed in a great smile. "I do many things these days I never used to do. For you, it is a pleasure."

He soon had the buggy ready. I got aboard, thanked him, slapped the reins and the horse moved off at a leisurely pace. I suspected that Mr. Lindsay had chosen a slow animal for me to drive, which was a wise gesture because I knew little about horses.

There was a fairly definable trail leading from the dirt road to the foot of the hillock atop which the ugly hulk squatted like some huge, evil creature keeping watch on everything below.

I left the buggy and found another vague trail up the slope. I followed it and soon discovered the gangplank. Now, I knew that when the packet was afire and people were dying there'd been no gangplank for the simple reason that there was no land for the far end of the plank to rest upon. Therefore, this slanting plank must have been put in place long after the destruction of the craft.

I stood quietly for a few moments examining the hulk at this close position. There wasn't much room for anything except the wreck on this knoll, and from where I stood I could look across our plantation and, by turning my head, see parts of the village far below. The packet had been driven quite a distance from the river during the storm when the crevasse carried the flood all the way across our plantation. This knoll, being the highest land point, was where the packet bogged down forever, high and dry when the waters subsided.

It was a large packet. The fire had not destroyed all of the jigsaw carpentry which made such elaborate and intricate work around the pilot house, resembling a gazebo at the rear of someone's estate.

I walked slowly up the sagging gangplank until I finally stepped onto the main deck. There was less damage by fire than I'd believed from my viewpoint as we drove pass it. The deck seemed intact and there was no danger of stepping on a weakened surface to have it break down under my feet.

The doors to the main cabin, the grand salon, had been torn away and probably wound up in the river. Through this great opening I could see all the way down the grand salon which extended almost the full length of this deck. It was the true centerpiece of the boat and had been heavily decorated. Now it was filled with a jumble of broken chairs and tables. About twenty brass spittoons were piled up haphazardly in a corner. At the far end of the salon, where the women passengers had best liked to congregate, there'd been a huge, ceiling-high mirror, now shattered.

My foot kicked green-molded silverware. There were some broken serving dishes, still stained with food. Apparently the packet was washed out of the river either just before or after the supper hour and the peak of the storm.

Some framed oils sagged against the walls, long since fallen from their proper places, and most were unrecognizable. I walked the full length of the salon and stopped to admire the sterling-silver water cooler. The silver cups, still on their chains, hung from the cooler. If this packet had been abandoned without its captain cursing everyone as he died, its contents would have been looted many years ago. Evidently nobody had the courage to come aboard.

Individual cabins were off the main salon and I pushed away the sagging door leading into one of them. I felt like crying, for it must have been so lovely here. Chairs, a table, and what was left of the bed lay in ruins, mostly in pieces, but the thick carpet on the floor hadn't burned. The windows were intact too, and were of stained glass, now so dirty it was impossible to even tell the colors. The ship must have been so lovely as it sailed serenely on its way down the river. And then the flood, the crevasse, the whirling, lunging packet carried on a wave of water over dry land to lodge here on the knoll while it burned and people died. With onlookers unable to help in any way, while the captain cursed all within the sound of his voice.

As I left this shattered cabin I thought I heard a faint creaking sound and I came to a dead stop. The sound was not repeated and I believed it came from the natural creaking of ancient, weathered wood. Yet I had the feeling that someone else was aboard. When I discovered I could not rid myself of this eerie sensation, I decided to leave the packet as quickly as possible.

I walked briskly along the main salon. Nearing the end of it where daylight beckoned me, I heard a distinct sound behind me and I turned in time to see a man bearing down on me.

I screamed and fled, but I wasn't fast enough. I had to be careful of where I stepped because of the debris that littered the deck. The man plunged on through it all and I felt my arm seized in a tight grasp. I was spun around. Two strong arms enveloped me, holding me firmly. Yet the terror I felt vanished as quickly as it came. The man who held me was about twenty-two, I judged. He had clear and blue eyes brimming with laughter and his smile was genuinely good humored. I knew instantly that there was nothing to fear from him.

"Please let go of me," I said sharply.

He promptly released me. "I'm sorry, Miss Carolyn, but I was afraid you were going to jump overboard and I wouldn't have wanted that pretty dress you're wearing to get dirty. I know I frightened you and I do beg your pardon."

"I should think you would," I said stiffly.

"Well, I did have cause to catch you. I didn't know who was prowling about and with the reputation this packet has I was not given to the taking of chances. Please let me introduce myself. I am Jeff Horton. I live in the village and I know your father very well."

"You certainly knew who I was when you addressed me by name."

"Everyone in the village knows you are back on the plantation with your mother. While I never set eyes on you before, I was told you were an extraordinarily attractive girl and, seeing that you are, I recognized you."

I straightened my somewhat wrinkled dress. "I am not impressed by your flattery, Mr. Horton. May I ask what you're doing aboard this hulk?"

"The same thing as you, Miss Carolyn. I'm trying to find out how a bell can ring when, actually, it can't be rung. And how a whistle blows when it's an impossibility."

"You have some connection with the packet?"

"Some. My mother was killed in the wreck and the fire."

I breathed deeply. "I'm sorry, Mr. Horton. I shouldn't have been so unpleasant. I am aboard for the same reason. My father lies desperately ill and he waits for that dreadful whistle to blow because it means he will soon die. It blew last evening, as you probably know, and a man died."

Mr. Horton nodded, somewhat curtly, I thought. "Yes. And there were many others before him. People who died without any known cause. Victims of what? Revenge? The vengeance of a captain dead for all these years and whose curse is supposed to still live? Do you believe that?"

I said, "No, I do not."

"Come with me," he said, and took my elbow. "I'll show you what I mean about the bell and the whistle."

He led me across the deck and up a short flight of steps to the top deck. We reached the pilothouse and he pointed to a large brass bell atop it. The metal was, in spots, green with the destruction that comes with time and exposure.

"Look at the rope by which the bell was rung. It's frayed and all but turned to dust. If that rope was pulled, it would disintegrate. Now, on the other corner of the wheelhouse, that broken, rusted-out tube of metal is the whistle. Even if there was a head of steam up, that whistle would burst if anyone attempted to blow it. I could show you the boilers too. There were four of them. Two blew up when the packet was stranded on the knoll. The other two are so rusted their sides are full of holes. You couldn't get up an ounce of steam in them."

"I do see what you mean," I said. "The bell cannot be rung and the whistle could not sound under any circumstances."

"Correct."

"Then what bell do we hear and what whistle blows?" I asked.

"I wish I knew," he said grimly. "I've been trying to find out. Three times, last night included, I drove up here as fast as I could urge my horse to run. I hoped I might find something, but . . . I did not. I inspected the wreck by lantern light and nobody had been aboard. I looked all about the knoll and discovered nothing."

"Yet a man did die and those sounds were heard."

"Yes, quite true. I wish there was something I could do about it."

We returned to the boiler deck and stood at the stern of the packet where the fire damage was less. I said, "I intend to find out what causes men to die this way. I will not leave until I know the answers."

"Why not, then, fight this thing together, Miss Carolyn?"

"Indeed, Mr. Horton, that would be a fine idea. After I make inquiries about you. As I may have said, I can't afford to take any chances. My father is dying."

He extended his hand and spoke gravely. "Ask whom

you will and what you will. When you are convinced I am neither addled, nor have any sinister connection with this, we shall then put our heads together and try to make some sense of this outrageous series of tragedies."

We left the ship. Mr. Horton had a horse tied to a tree close by. I'd missed seeing the animal because it was hidden by tall brush. He escorted me to my buggy.

"Please let me know as soon as you're satisfied with me, Miss Carolyn."

"I feel that I can trust you now," I said.

I liked the gentle way about this man and yet I knew he could be strong and tough when he wanted to be. He was the kind of a man I could instinctively have faith in. He was taller than I by a good eight inches and he was rangy looking. His smile was infectious and his sincerity so warm it was certainly genuine.

"Thank you for that," he said. "I've long wished I had someone to join in my efforts to solve this mystery. Whenever I broached the subject, my audience vanished like a puff of smoke. Everyone in the village is convinced the packet is the home of all the ghosts of those who died that terrible night. They regard the captain's curse as a living thing that will exist until the last soul coming under the curse is dead and the ghosts satisfied."

"Then may we soon convince those poor benighted people they are wrong, Mr. Horton."

"Do you know, Miss Carolyn, I'm beginning to think we will."

"Good, sir. Confidence in ourselves will help, I'm sure."

"When may I call upon you?"

"Whenever you wish. Perhaps we can talk to my father. He may have an idea or two, though he is sometimes too ill to be questioned. Yet, I'm sure if we go at this business in the proper way we will find the answers."

He helped me into the buggy and I drove off only to find him soon riding beside the buggy. Nearing the road to the plantation, he trotted on ahead and turned off in the direction of the village. I found myself smiling slightly over the idea that we might work together. He wasn't as handsome or as suave as Dr. Shea, for instance, but he was far more intelligent and gentlemanly than Randy Austin, who had met us at the dock.

Yvonne came out to meet me and said she would fetch Mr. Lindsay to put the buggy away. I went on into the house and straight up to papa's room. He was wide awake and reached out a hand toward me. I sat down and held his hand in my own.

"Your mother is lying down," he said. "She was up with me all night and she's exhausted."

"Then I should have been here to take her place," I said. "I'm sorry I was not."

"It's all right. Yvonne looks after me very well. I'm glad you're back, Carolyn. There were times when I wondered if I really did have a beautiful daughter."

"You should have allowed mama and me to stay here on the plantation."

"No. You see what's happening to me. That's bad enough, but if it ever happened to you or your mother I'd have blamed myself."

"I've been aboard the wreck, papa."

"I thought as much. I went aboard her a hundred times and found nothing."

"I found Jeff Horton aboard," I said.

"What was he doing there?" papa asked quickly.

"For the same reason. Trying to find some answers. Needless to say, we didn't. Mr. Horton is determined to solve this thing, papa, and I want to help him do it. But first I have to be sure he can be trusted."

"He didn't tell you, then?"

"Tell me what?" I asked.

"It was his father who died last night. The bell and the whistle sounded for him."

I brought my hands to my face quickly. "Oh, papa, I didn't know. I'm so ashamed of myself."

"You only arrived yesterday," he reminded me. "You don't know anyone here. So how would you be expected to be aware of Jeff's grief? I can say this much for the young man. I know of nobody any finer, as to his character and his habits. He is a cotton broker with an office in New Orleans, but since his father's illness he has spent all his time here."

"Then I will gladly work with him if he'll have me after that awful lack of knowledge about his father. I must confess, I like the man."

"Better than Dr. Shea, perhaps?" he asked with a twinkle in his eyes that reminded me of times long gone by.

"Oh, papa, I like Dr. Shea too. In fact he gave me to understand that he will call upon me. So did Randy Austin, for that matter."

"Boyd Shea is a highly respected young man and a good doctor. Randy—well, I don't think he's quite grown up yet. He'll do, in a few more years."

I wanted to abandon that subject. I said, "Papa, do you have any idea at all about what's been happening here?"

"I wish I did, Carolyn. My very life seems to depend on it, but I have no answers."

"The bell cannot be rung; the whistle can't be sounded. I refuse to believe in ghosts, so there has to be an answer somewhere."

"If there is it has eluded me for ten years. After you hear the bell and the whistle time after time, during all those years, you don't know what to think and your mind goes off in a dozen directions."

"Does it appear to be some scheme inspired only by revenge? Could there be some survivor of the wreck, or some close relative to one of the victims, who is doing this out of vengeance?"

"It's the only theory that makes any sense, though I have toyed with another."

"Tell me, papa, please," I begged.

"This applies only to me, not to any of the other victims, which makes it a weak idea, to say the least. If someone wanted to take this plantation away from me, this is the best way to do it. I can't keep any help, except a very few loyal people. I haven't profited any in five years.

For the last three I've kept the place going at a great loss and before too long I won't be able to keep the place at all."

"Is anyone after it?"

"It has been one of the most prosperous plantations in the state, Carolyn. Almost anyone would covet it, but I can't point a finger of suspicion at anybody who would go to these extremes to get it."

"Is there anyone in particular?" I persisted in my questioning of him.

"Randy's father made me an offer about a year ago. A ridiculous one, though he pointed out that he would have to assume all the fear I was experiencing, for he would gain possession of the wrecked packet along with the plantation and, so he maintained, the ghosts would then turn their attenion to him. He made it a selling point. I might be able to get away from the evil influence of the ghosts by selling out."

"Anyone else in particular?"

"Not that I can seriously consider. There have been no other real offers."

"I'll speak to Jeff about this. If you don't mind."

"Go right ahead, my dear. I might remind you the funeral of his father is this afternoon."

I arose hastily. "Then I must dress, for I intend to go and to apologize to him for my thoughtlessness. I'll waken mama before I leave. I do hope you are feeling stronger."

"I'm all right," he assured me. "Run along. Work with Jeff. You might even save my life."

I cried out in anguish over his predicament and I kissed him before I dried my few tears and left. I had no mourning clothes so I had to make do with a dark brown dress and a plain straw hat. I left off all jewelry, as was the custom. I had Calvin Lindsay harness the buggy again

"I'm going to Mr. Horton's funeral," I said.

"I am too," he told me. "But later. A sad thing, Miss Carolyn. Did you know the man?"

"I don't remember him, but I met his son Jeff this morning."

"A likable lad, that one. Coming along fine, he is. For a motherless son, he's doing well, I must say. His mother died on the packet, you know."

"Yes, he mentioned it. Yet his father seems to have fallen victim to this strange curse. Isn't that unusual? Jeff's father should have been regarded as having suffered enough."

"Aye, but the curse does strange things, miss. Yet Jeff's father was never bitter, claiming it was all by accident and none should be held to blame."

He helped me into the buggy. "Thank you," I said. "One thing more, Mr. Lindsay. Do you think we can work together and restore this plantation? Make it pay again? Show a profit?"

He regarded me most seriously. "You're like your pa, Miss Carolyn. Takes someone with brains to run the place. I got the muscle, but I'm not so good at figuring things. Together we just might make it go, and if you're willing, I sure am."

"Fine. We'll talk later. If we could get this place running well it would do a great deal to help papa's condition."

He almost shook his head in negative fashion but caught himself in time. He didn't comment, but I knew what he would have said. That by the time the plantation would be on its feet again, papa would be long dead. I knew that too, but I was afraid to accept the truth for fear that it would prove too discouraging. The best thing I could do, for myself, mama and papa, was to go ahead as if I expected no disaster.

Meantime, I had a funeral to attend, so I headed the buggy toward the village. It was a sad occasion. I would be glad to see Jeff and to apologize for my ignorance of his loss. This way I might cheer him somewhat.

Nearing the dirt road I came into full view of that ominous hulk astride the knoll, surveying everything as if it were alive, and gloating over the despair once again cast upon the villagers because another victim had been claimed by a fifteen-year-old curse.

FIVE

The village had a population of slightly more than three hundred, I had learned, and all but a handful were either inside or outside the white-painted church. As I felt myself a comparative stranger here, I made no attempt to enter, believing that those who knew Jeff's father best had preference. I did see Calvin Lindsay use his massive shoulders to make way through the crowd at the door and enter himself.

The glass-enclosed hearse with its draped windows and its four black-plumed horses waited outside. After the services, Jeff followed the coffin alone. He rode a hack behind the hearse, again alone, and the village followed in a motly assortment of vehicles. I brought up almost at the rear.

The village graveyard was but a ten-minute ride. There I watched the graveside services being held. Everyone was dressed in black, except for me and a bent old crone who, I would have judged, would always wear black. Instead, she was in a white dress, more like an improbable bride than a mourner. She remained well away from the graveside. An enormous white hat, decorated with egret feathers, was atop her head, making her look even more ridiculous. I wondered who in the world she might be. And why she attended a funeral dressed gaily in white.

Once she looked my way and our eyes locked for an instant before she bent her head quickly, but I could have sworn I saw the beginning of a smile on her face. For some reason she made me shiver, though the afternoon was hot and sultry. When I looked again, she was gone. How she had disappeared so quickly—and completely—I had no idea, but I couldn't find any trace of her in the crowd. Not even after the service was over and I, among many others, approached Jeff to offer my condolences.

"I'm truly sorry," I told him when my turn came. "I had no idea it was your father who died."

"There is no need to feel badly about that," he said. "In fact, I will forgive you if you let me ride back in your buggy. I shall dismiss the hack, if you will be so kind."

"Of course," I said. "I'll wait for you."

Presently he joined me and we headed back toward the village, but halfway there I pulled over beneath the shade of a great oak, dripping with Spanish moss. Here there was a breath of cool air.

"Mr. Horton—"I began.

"Please, my name is Jeff, and we are friends, I hope."

"Jeff then. I noticed a strange woman at the services. She must be seventy or more, a bent over figure dressed all in white. Who is she? And why does she attend a funeral dressed that way?"

He laughed shortly. "That would be Hattie. We don't know anything else about her, neither where she came from nor how she manages to live without an income that anyone is aware of. She has a small cottage, lives alone and minds her own business in the strictest fashion. Until there is a funeral of someone under the curse. She always goes, and she always dresses in white."

"Do you think she gets some personal satisfaction in attending funerals?"

"Yes, I do. And I also think someone she loved died aboard the packet. She came four or five years after the packet burned. She just appeared one day, bought the cottage and paid cash for it. She settled down and has lived there ever since. I doubt she goes out, except to buy what little she requires to keep body and soul together, and to attend the funerals of those who died to the note of the steamboat whistle."

"She won't explain anything?" I asked.

"She barred her door many years ago and she speaks to

no one unless it is absolutely necessary. I tried to talk to her several times and she walked away from me. Or kept her door bolted if I called upon her."

"In my opinion," I said, "she took a weird delight in the funeral of your father. To my mind, that means she certainly knows something about the curse. Oh, Jeff, I'm sorry. To be talking this way right after . . . your loss. I should have known better."

"Your own father is desperately ill, as mine was. I think we should not only talk about doing something, but plan to track down this mystery. At once, Carolyn. There are many others who fall under the curse. If matters hold true to their course, now that my father is dead, and your father probably the next to die, another will become ill. It's always been like that. I think the villagers are affected by this series of events more than by the actual deaths. It's as if the curse is a living one that never ceases, never tires and cannot be stopped."

"We dare not delay, Jeff. We must try to do something at once."

"Where to begin? I've asked myself a dozen times what I might be able to do and nothing comes to mind. We're dealing with something that began years ago. It appears to be the work of ghosts, or a curse so strong it has lasted all this time and still exacts its toll."

"It begins," I said, "with survivors of the wreck who lost relatives or loved ones. With villagers, or with people from other places who also suffered losses. If this is a matter of revenge, then the blame for all this must rest with someone who seeks vengeance. Are there any survivors who escaped the fire?"

"Two. Willie Spencer, a recluse who lives a life even more secluded than the woman in white. He seems to be an educated man who spends his time reading, sometimes hiking through the meadows or dozing with a fishing rod on the banks of the river. He appears to be harmless, though very reticent. He lost his wife in the wreck."

"And the other?" I asked.

"Edward Baker. He lost his wife and two children and, like Willie Spencer, barely escaped with his own life. He was dreadfully burned and bears scars that have disfigured him to such an extent that he has been slowly drinking himself to death. Unsuccessfully, I might add, for he seems to have the stamina of a younger man. He has a hut near the cemetery and is found at the graves of his family as often as in the tavern. He used to be, according to what I have learned about him, a very forceful man with great ambitions. Now he has none and he hates everyone because they have not been as unfortunate as he."

"They sound to me like very unlikely people to keep this series of deaths going, but I suppose one can never tell what such men are really made of."

"I have been suspicious of both, though I have yet to discover anything to verify my suspicions."

"And the woman in white?" I asked. "Haven't you also suspected her?"

"Oh, yes. However, in her case I don't see how she could manage to create sounds that resemble a ship's bell and a ship's whistle. Possibly the men might have discovered some way to create these sounds, but not the old lady."

"We don't seem to be getting very far, Jeff," I remarked.

"I've been trying to for at least ten years and especially so since my father became ill a year ago and I knew he was going to die like all the others. You can almost prophesy when these illnesses begin and when they . . . end."

"How much time do you give my father?"

"Perhaps a month or two."

"Jeff, have all these deaths been due to the same strange illness?"

"No, there were three or four instances when the victim was killed apparently by accident, but the whistle always blew."

I was thinking about this while I completed the ride to the village, where Jeff got off.

"May I call on you soon?" he asked.

"At any time you wish, Jeff. I shall always be glad to see you."

"Thank you. I have some business details to finish. Perhaps this evening? . . ."

"I'll look forward to it."

He glanced up at me. "I shall be calling so we may discuss our course of action, but that is not the main reason. I want to see you because . . . I'm falling in love with you."

He turned and walked rapidly away before I could comment. I watched his lean body as he moved with long, strong steps. I had an urge to call his name loudly, to get him back to my side, but this was no time for it. He'd just buried his father and his mind must be filled with many thoughts and so much sadness.

I had no intention of spurning the love he had offered so abruptly and unexpectedly, for I had liked him from the start. I would anxiously wait for him to call tonight. But I would give him no direct answer to any profession of his love for me. Before I would allow myself to even consider anything else, I had to save my father's life. I must get the plantation back in order and I must, somehow, determine who, or what, lay behind this campaign of frightfulness and death.

I left the village and proceeded at a pace which I let the horse assume. I was so immersed in my thoughts that when the horse suddenly gave a scream and rose up on its hind legs, I was totally unprepared. The buggy almost tipped over, the reins were wrenched from my hand and the horse began to run, assuming top speed in less than a minute. I had to use both hands to hang on so I wouldn't be thrown clear. The horse, still alarmed for some unknown reason, left the dirt road and pulled the buggy over flat land where saw grass had grown high. The tough grass scraped at the horse's legs and made him all the more unruly. I was in a runaway buggy and helpless, for I didn't even have the reins in hand and I was unable to reach for them without letting go of the side of the buggy.

Then the inevitable happened. The horse, trying to avoid an especially formidable display of saw grass, made a violent turn. The buggy rocked on two wheels and finally threw me out. I landed amidst the grass and the wind was knocked out of me so that I was unable to move. The coarse grass had already torn the flesh on my hands and face. I pulled myself into a sitting position. I was still too dazed to know whether or not I'd been more seriously hurt. I found out when I tried to stand. My ankle gave way under me and a wave of excruciating pain shot up my leg. My ankle was either badly sprained or broken. I didn't know which, but in either case, I could put no weight on it.

I was a hundred or more yards from the road. It was infrequently traveled, I already knew, and to wait here on the chance that someone would ride by seemed foolish to me. There was a chance I might be more seriously injured than I now believed and I was in need of medical attention.

The horse had come to a stop the moment the buggy righted itself after pitching me out. I called to the animal, but the mare didn't move except to shiver visibly from fright or pain. Saw grass can be cruel to animals as well as humans.

Hopping on one foot, I slowly made my way toward the buggy. As I neared it, I began talking to the horse, trying to calm her so she wouldn't bolt again. I reached the buggy and crawled into it, with perspiration pouring down my face from the humid heat of the afternoon and the agony from my ankle. I was sure it must be broken.

I kept a tight hold on the reins and I managed to guide the horse out of the saw grass. Once clear of it, the mare settled down and we made the rest of the trip without incident. When I pulled up in front of the plantation house, I saw Calvin Lindsay down by the stable and I called to him. He must have recognized the note of urgency in my voice, for he came at a run.

"I was thrown out of the buggy," I explained. "I'm afraid my ankle is broken. Please help me into the house and then see to the horse. She may be injured too."

Calvin needed no further instructions. He was a practical man in all things. He reached into the buggy, lifted me, cradled me in his arms and marched toward the house. Yvonne must have seen us approaching, for she came out in a hurry and grew most excited and concerned about my injury. I was placed on a sofa in the living room and while Calvin went out to care for the horse, Yvonne helped me remove my dress and get into a robe. Mama, called from her room by Yvonne, was too agitated to help much.

"Everything about this house," she said, "the plantation and the village as well, means only sorrow and trouble. I hate it here."

"Now, mama," I said. "It's a pleasant village and the people are very kind. It's not the plantation or this house which is to blame, but someone who hates us and everyone who saw the packet burn."

"I cannot believe you were injured purely by accident," she said.

"Mama, nobody was anywhere near me. I was driving alone on the road from the village. Something made the horse bolt—"

"Something? That's just it! We don't know what this something is, but it brings death and disaster. Your father is no better. If we could persuade him to go to New Orleans, away from all this . . . these supernatural happenings. . . ."

"Mama," I said, "he would never leave the plantation, and you know it. He's had years to get away if he wished, but he never will. Trying to change his mind will only worsen his condition."

"I suppose so," she conceded finally. "But I do wish there was something we could do. For myself, I'm terrified every day I'm here. Imagine, a ghost exacting vengeance over a period of so many years."

"I refuse to believe it is a ghost," I said. "Nor do I think a curse can turn into reality. There is more behind it than that. Only vengeance perhaps, but not caused by a curse or the activities of a ghost."

"I even dislike talking about it. Does your ankle give you much pain?"

"Yes," I admitted. "It's very painful."

Fortunately Calvin Lindsay came in to end this unsatisfactory conversation with mama. He presented me with a stout cane. "I've had this for years. Busted my own ankle once and the cane was very useful. Tell me, Miss Carolyn, what happened to make the horse bolt?"

"I don't know, Mr. Lindsay."

"Did you use the whip on her?"

"I've never used a whip," I said. "The mare was just jogging along. I wasn't pressing her. All of a sudden she reared up and then bolted, right off the road into that awful saw grass."

"She was cut up some by it, but there's something else. Was anybody near you when this happened?"

"I don't know what you mean. I was riding alone. . . ."

"There's a welt on the side of the mare's neck. A great big one. She was hit by something. It wasn't a bullet because the skin was barely broken, but it hit with great force."

"I saw no one. There was no other vehicle on the road. . . ."

"Got me an idea what caused it, only it sounds a little crazy."

"Please," I said, "tell me. Never mind how crazy it sounds."

"Well, the way I see it, this was caused by a stone. It couldn't have been thrown, because whoever threw it would have had to be close to the horse and you'd have seen who it was. Besides, nobody could throw a stone with such force, so I think somebody was hiding in the brush near the road and used a slingshot to hurt the horse. Whoever it was knew darned well the horse would rear up and likely run away. It looks to me like somebody was set on hurting you, Miss Carolyn."

"We should go away from here," mama said. "We should not spend another day in this house—"

"Mama, I'm not leaving and papa won't leave either. Besides, Mr. Lindsay and I are going to put this plantation back into running order before we lose everything."

"My dear," mama said, "do you know what may happen? . . ."

"I know, and I'm not going to allow myself to be afraid. Mr. Lindsay, will you be so kind as to ride to the village and ask Dr. Shea to attend me. If the ankle is broken, I wish to know it before I try to stand up and put weight upon the limb."

"I'll go at once," he said. "About the plantation. I got some ideas we can talk about later."

"If the ankle is broken we'll likely have plenty of time to talk about your ideas," I said.

"I'll be as fast as possible," he assured me, and he left the house promptly. Minutes later I heard him ride by.

Mama was still worried, still anxious to get away from this trouble and sorrow. "I'm not a selfish woman," she said. "I love your father dearly, but if he remains stubborn about leaving—to save his own life, really—I don't see what good I can do here. I'm not up to facing these tragedies and I'm frightened. I'm also worried about you, my dear."

"Why don't you go back to New Orleans, mama? As you say, there is little you can do except be a comfort to papa."

"I'm anything but that. He knows how worried and afraid I am, and he has asked me to go back. And to take you with me, I might add."

"No, mama. I won't leave. There are things I can do here—many things—but especially I can try to find out who is causing these deaths. There's the plantation to think of as well. We have lived off it, luxuriously, I will admit, and if it isn't kept up we're going to have to adjust to a far smaller income. So I'm going to stay and put the farm back on its feet. Get the sugar house running again."

"How? Nobody will work here. Your father said so."

"Perhaps we can persuade them otherwise," I said. "When you are ready, I'll help you pack and Mr. Lindsay will take you to the dock where he can signal a packet to pick you up."

Mama shook her head. "If you remain, there's all the more reason why I should. I'm a bit addled, I suppose, because of all this fear, but my place is with my husband and I will stay. I hope I won't become too great a burden on you. I'll do my best not to be."

"Oh, mama, you're not a burden. You'll help a great deal by caring for papa so I can devote my time to the plantation. If we get it going again, papa will take courage from that, I know. Thank you for changing your mind."

"I should have been spanked for even thinking about leaving. I'm going back to your father now. When the doctor comes, I'll be down again to help, if I can."

"Good. I'll appreciate it."

Halfway across the room, she stopped and turned around. "What shall I tell your father about the accident?"

"Just say that's what it was, an accident. Tell him some wild animal must have crossed in front of the horse without my seeing it. As soon as the doctor arrives and treats my ankle, I'll be up myself. Tell him that too."

Mama nodded. "I wish I had your courage. I'm proud of you, Carolyn. You never had to fend for yourself before and you're so good at it."

"I haven't been harmed by it, mama," I said. "I'm ashamed of the selfishness I showed before we came back home. This is our home now. I love it here and you will too, when we rid ourselves of this weird curse, or whatever it is."

SIX

Dr. Shea rode so fast from the village that he reached the plantation before Cal Lindsay. Yvonne, on the lookout for him, led him into the living room where I sat with my legs stretched out on the sofa. While he made a swift and professional examination of the ankle, I told him what had happened and about Cal's theory that the horse had been deliberately excited by a painful blow from a stone, hurled by a slingshot.

Dr. Shea began unrolling a bandage. "First of all, the ankle. It's not broken. There's a bad sprain and it will have to be strapped for some time. Stay off it as much as possible for a couple of days and be sure to use the cane when you do move about."

"Thank heaven no bones were broken," I said.

"You're lucky, because judging from the nature of the sprain, it almost came to broken bones. Now, I'm going to have a look at the mare. Cal suggested it, but if Cal says the mare was hit by a stone, I won't doubt him. He knows far more about animals wounds than I. Rest here. I'll be back soon."

Yvonne sat down in her usual graceful way. "I am sorry, *mademoiselle,* that you have been injured, but it was bound to happen. *Oui,* it is surprising it was no worse."

"Yvonne, what do you mean by saying it was bound to happen?"

"It is the curse, *mademoiselle.* It was a curse cast upon those who would not help when the packet burned, and upon their loved ones as well. Many of those who died had close kin who have been often hurt by accident. It's all part of the curse."

"You do believe that, don't you, Yvonne?"

"I would not say all this if I did not believe. *Oui,* it is hard for one raised as you in a big city to believe these things, but they are true. I have seen curses work before. There is no way to break them until the reason for the curse itself is exhausted. That means when the last person bound to suffer under the curse is dead."

"You learned of these matters in Jamaica, Yvonne?"

"They were taught me as a child," she replied simply.

"If it is true," I said, "I'm going to break that curse. Somehow I'll find the way to do it. Doesn't the curse frighten you? So many others have left the plantation. Why not you?"

"The curse is not directed at me. I am safe and without fear for myself. I was not even here. I fear for you and your mama, and your papa. It is common knowledge that at the time of the fire and the bursting crevasse, your father was the most important man watching the packet as it burned. Had he given orders, perhaps a few might have been saved. But he gave no orders. He did nothing to inspire others to try and save those aboard."

"Yvonne, it would have been impossible to save anyone. My father knew that and gave no orders because they would have only resulted in further loss of life. This I know from what has been told me by others who were there."

"Oui, it is true. But those on the packet did not know this. They believed an attempt should have been made. I know that they could not be helped, but had I been on one of the decks, and my life in terrible danger, I might have thought something could have been done. At the time of the fire it depended on where you stood. Your papa made all this clear to me."

"That is a wise and generous observation, Yvonne. I'm grateful for it. Yet I can't believe in curses, nor in vengeance sought by persons who are dead. Mr. Lindsay and I intend to get the plantation going again."

"Bon, it is good to do this. I too will help whenever I can. Once it was a great place, with all hands busily at work, and all were happy. It has been my wish this would again take place. But, *mademoiselle,* you will have to do it all without the help of your papa."

"I know that. Until he becomes well again he can only advise, but that will help."

"No, *mademoiselle.* Your papa, he will not live much longer. This I feel. In my bones I feel it. The curse is still strong and it will take him as it took others. Nothing can prevent this."

"Something can if it is done in time," I challenged her belief. "And I would consider it a favor if you would not make such statements to anyone else, especially to mama, and certainly never to my father."

"To you only I tell the truth as I see it, *mademoiselle.* There are certain things I may do as well. I shall attend to that at once. I am not against you, *mademoiselle.* I am on your side."

"Thank you, Yvonne." I wondered what she meant by certain things she could do. There wouldn't have been time to ask her for an explanation if I had decided to, for Dr. Shea returned just then and came at once to my side.

"I agree with Calvin. The horse was injured by some kind of a missile, likely a stone. And the idea that it was done with the use of a slingshot is also quite possible. Now I shall visit your father for a time. I need not ask if you will be here when I come down again. It would not be wise to move any more than you have to."

Before Dr. Shea had finished with papa, Jeff arrived, also in great haste, for he'd heard the news which Calvin had apparently spread through the village.

"I'm so sorry this happened," he said. "I should have ridden back with you."

"Then we both might have been hurt, Jeff. Don't blame this on yourself."

"You saw no one?"

"Not a soul. The grass is high on both sides of the road and there is thick forest close by as well. Anyone could have hidden there."

"He had to know you were on your way home," Jeff said thoughtfully. "You could have been seen leaving the village. If you drove slowly a man on horseback could have passed you without your knowing it and then waited for you to pass."

"Jeff, what reason could there be for anyone to desire me hurt or dead?"

"I don't know. That's the trouble. We don't know, or even have an idea of who is behind this. Perhaps that person thought you were going to interfere with his plans and decided to create an accident where you too would be killed."

I pounded the cane on the floor with each word. "Why? Why? Why?"

"The curse," Jeff said.

"I can't make myself believe it."

"Nor I, but there seems to be no other answer. You're sure the ankle is not broken?"

"Ask Carolyn's doctor." Dr. Shea had made his way quite noiselessly down the stairs and into the living room. He startled me, though Jeff didn't seem affected.

"Hello, Doctor." Jeff stood up and offered his hand. "I am asking you."

"She'll be fine in a few days. A nasty sprain, but it will heal quickly enough. I found your father quite well, Carolyn. Surprisingly so. I thought he was strong enough to hear about your accident. That's what I made it out to be, a simple accident and nothing else."

"Thank you for telling him," I said. "He'd have found out soon anyway and now I don't have to make any extended explanations."

"And Eric's condition?" Jeff inquired.

"As I said, quite good."

"Does that mean he will get well?" Jeff persisted.

Dr. Shea betrayed a bit of annoyance. "I didn't say that, only that he seemed more cheerful and somewhat improved."

"I see. In other words, there is no fundamental change?"

Shea laughed curtly. He was annoyed and showed it even more. "That's well put, sir. No significant change."

"Thank you," Jeff said. "I only wanted it straight in my mind."

"Of course, Jeff. Carolyn, may I call this evening?"

"I'd be delighted," I said.

"I thought I'd stay," Jeff said quietly.

"You're welcome to," I told him, somewhat enjoying the rivalry of these two men.

"Then you won't ride back with me, Jeff?"

"No, Doctor. I've matters to talk over. About the plantation. Cal Lindsay has agreed to join us. We're going to try and get the place running again."

"That's a worthy idea," Dr. Shea commented. "If there is anything I can do, let me know."

"Of course," Jeff said, with the air of a man who'd never need help—especially not from Dr. Shea.

I experimented in limping about and finally made it all the way to where Dr. Shea's horse was tied.

"Jeff," he said, "is a pleasant young man and quite successful. Or he has been up to now. If he disregards his New Orleans office much longer, he'll need a job on your plantation. I shall return this evening, unless an emergency comes up. That is always a hazard to a doctor when he looks forward to a pleasant evening."

He rode away and Jeff came out to help me limp back to the house. At least I could move about and not suffer too much pain, though I was glad to ease myself down on the sofa once more.

"I must see papa soon," I said.

"Yes, I realize that," Jeff said. "I'll go down to the stable and find Lindsay. Maybe we can plan some kind of a start with the plantation. And I want to look over the sugar house and the crop, if there is any."

"Please join me at supper. Mama will likely have her supper upstairs with papa and we might get a little work done."

Jeff did help me up the stairs, which was rather difficult until I grew accustomed to them. Fortunately, the use of the cane helped support my injured ankle.

Papa managed a wan smile as I crossed the room to his side. "You haven't had what could be called a glorious reception on your homecoming," he said. "I hope you're not in too much pain."

"Oh, papa, it's nothing. A sprained ankle, that's all. I'll be fine in no time. But how are you? Dr. Shea said there seemed to be some improvement."

"Perhaps. Not much, as I judge it. Having you back is a tonic in itself. How did the accident happen?"

"I'm not sure. I think some animal crossed the road in front of the mare and frightened her into bolting. I can't account for it in any other way."

"You're likely right. That mare always was a mite skittish. What do you think of our doctor, now that you know him better?"

"I like the man. He's handsome and very clever, I think."

"And Jeff Horton?"

"He may be a New Orleans cotton broker, but he's certainly not out of place on a plantation. We're going to start work on this one right away and we'll need a great deal of advice from you, papa."

"I won't run away from it," he said with a smile. "I

look forward to being useful, even if in only a small way. It will be interesting as well . . . to see what happens."

" 'What happens'? Papa, you mean the plantation? . . ."

"I mean Dr. Shea and Jeff Horton. They're both shiny eyed whenever they look at you or talk about you."

"Papa, I barely know them."

"That doesn't mean a thing."

I quickly changed the subject and we talked mostly about the sugar house and how to put it back into shape. The last papa knew, nothing was rusted. Calvin and three or four men who didn't abandon the plantation kept the machinery in order and the plant was ready to resume operations as quickly as the crop could be brought in. That was where the problem lay. Nobody wanted to work here. They were afraid of that curse. Not that I blamed them, after what had happened.

Our cook had left, but Yvonne was a wonderful cook and she prepared a fine supper, not even showing any temperament when a meal planned for Jeff and me turned out to have three more mouths to feed. Randy Austin, Anse, his father, and his mother, Marie, all came to ask about papa and naturally I had to invite them to stay. They visited with papa until supper was ready and they did help to cheer him up. Mama still insisted on having her supper in papa's room so that the conversation at the table turned from papa's condition and the effects of the curse—which all of the Austins believed in thoroughly—to the plantation.

Anse said, "I don't like talking about the farm and money while your pa is so sick. I do not like to offend people or bring them a moment of unhappiness. That's why I left the packet after I found out you and your ma were aboard. I didn't want to be asked how your father was."

"He's too sensitive a man," Marie said.

"He sure ain't when he's giving orders." Randy tried to inject a note of cheer into the conversation.

"What I'm getting at," Anse said, "is simple. I want to buy your pa's plantation, sugar house, mansion and all. I'll pay a fine price for it because this is valuable property.

Only it has to be kept going so it won't rot. I'm willing to talk business at any time."

"Please, Mr. Austin—" I began.

He held up a hand to silence me. "On the other hand, I know you don't want to sell. Leastwise, not yet. So, if you keep it and want to get it going again, I'll pitch in too."

"That's wonderful," I said.

"Just how?" Jeff asked, being far more practical.

"My hands don't mind working for me. They don't want to work here on account of that dead captain's curse on any who do—"

"Just a moment, please," I said. "What makes you say they are afraid to work here? Because the curse applies only to people who do work here?"

"Oh, no! No, not at all," Anse hastened to reply. "But as he shouted the curse the captain did mention your pa by name and also the plantation. As if they were to blame for it all, which your pa wasn't. Any more than I was."

Yvonne had appeared as Anse spoke, and she poured a small glass of brandy for Jeff and Randolph Austin. Anse turned his glass upside-down.

"Now that I don't like it, mind you, Yvonne. I do, and maybe too much. But I got me something burning inside my stomach. Forget what Doc Shea called it, but I can't drink anymore and I have to be careful of what I eat. I even had to give up my plug of tobacco, which was the hardest thing of all."

"He's got an ulcer," Marie said. "Had it a long time, but it seems to give him more trouble lately."

"And nothing can be done for it," Anse said bitterly.

"Well," Jeff said, "we'll certainly take you up on your offer to help. If your men have time on their hands, you might assign them to come over here and begin cutting the crop. What do you pay them, by the way?"

"Dollar and a quarter a day. That's pretty good wages."

"Tell them if they work here whenever you can spare them, we'll pay two dollars a day," Jeff said.

I hastily intervened. "Mr. Austin, that offer is high because they should be paid extra if they work in a place they fear. After a while they'll come to realize there's no harm here and then we'll adjust things. We don't want to take your help away from you."

"Ain't likely you could," Anse replied. "But they'll be glad to pick up a few extra dollars a week, and maybe if they stay on here long enough they'll get the other loafers in town to think twice about such foolishness as being afraid. The curse is meant only for those who watched the packet burn and didn't try to save anybody."

"Calvin and I will be on hand tomorrow," Jeff said. "I'll ask around town too, and see if I can find a few more to come out."

As we completed the meal, Dr. Shea drove up. Yvonne admitted him and he asked for a cup of coffee as he joined us at the table.

He waved a warning finger at Anse Austin. "You've been drinking coffee, Anse. I told you not to. Stick to milk. We've found that helps, and coffee and even tea are not good. You can't afford to take any chances."

"Once in a while—" Anse began.

Marie broke in. "I'll see that he drinks only milk, Doctor. He's stubborn, but not crazy. He knows he'll get pain if he doesn't take your advice and your medicine."

"The last batch was mighty bitter," Anse complained good-naturedly. "Can't you flavor it with a little whiskey?"

It turned out to be a pleasant evening. Jeff and Dr. Shea seemed to get along well and I gave no special favor to either one of them. I thought Randy looked a bit angry because they were there, and he watched me to a point where it was sometimes embarrassing. If anyone else noticed this, they made no remarks.

Finally the Austins left, and Dr. Shea followed soon after, for he had a patient he still had to see before he retired. Jeff was left and we sat side by side on the sofa. I liked the nearness of him and I liked the way he conducted himself with the others. He was a warm and friendly person.

"I told you, not too long ago, that I was falling in love with you," he said. "You didn't answer at the time and I can't blame you. I must have sounded a little foolish for making such a remark when I'd just come from the grave-side services for my father. But I meant it."

"Jeff, I have my troubles too. Let's not add to them now. Not that being in love with you would be trouble. Of course I didn't mean that, but my head is full of figures and plans for the plantation, and worries and hopes for my father."

"When I tell you this again," he said, "the plantation will be running and all its problems solved. And that curse will be exposed for what it really is: a fake. The work of someone who uses it to cover up his own selfish scheming."

"Thank you, Jeff. Will you be here in the morning?"

"At sunup. Cal and I are going to try and get the sugar mill running right off. It'll be ready when the crop starts coming in. And I'm going to hire Luke Bradley to supervise the sugaring. He's an expert at crystallization, but he's a frightened man and it'll take some talking to get him here. Talking and maybe five dollars a day. Unheard of, but he's worth it and we can't operate without him."

"Good," I said. "I leave all these matters up to you and I trust your judgment about finances. I'll ask papa, of course, for his approval, but I'm sure he'll see things our way too."

"Give me three months," Jeff vowed, "and this place will be alive again and turning out sugar and syrup as fast as it did before your pa got sick."

"I'm going through the cane fields in the morning," I said. "I want to get used to the work and be able to judge when the cane is just right for harvest."

"It is now. Maybe a mite too late," Jeff said. "We haven't had much rain and the fields are too dry. But Cal says we're in time, so everything will turn out fine."

"I shall be indebted to you for the rest of my life," I told him. "No one could be kinder."

"It's not all kindness," he said with more than a trace of bitterness. "I buried my pa. I think he died needlessly to satisfy someone's desire for revenge. I'm not going to stop until I find out who was responsible. It may take a long time, but I'll not be satisfied until I know the truth. Working here with you puts me close to the wreck and the curse. I want it that way because the closer I am, the better my chances of discovering what I'm after."

SEVEN

I awoke stiff and sore next morning. My ankle throbbed and only the tight bandage Dr. Shea had applied kept it from being even more painful. I dressed, being abnormally slow about it, for I had to balance myself on one foot half of the time. I used the cane and hobbled downstairs. I looked in on papa first but he was asleep and mama was in her own room, having been up most of the night with him.

Yvonne had a substantial breakfast ready and she fussed about because I wasn't eating enough. Finally I managed to make my slow way down to the edge of the cane fields. I had no idea how many arpents of cane were standing, but I knew this was a large plantation and unless work was begun soon, the crop would be a total loss.

Cal Lindsay, riding between the rows of cane on a sleek-looking horse, saw me and galloped in my direction. He swung out of the saddle and stood beside me surveying the tall cane. I could understand the pride I saw on his face, for it was going to be a good crop, assuming our ability to get it turned into juice. He was so impressed with the prospects, he didn't think to ask about my injury.

"Got eighty men coming out," he said. "We'll get the crop in, Miss Carolyn, sure as we're standing here. And we'll seed another for next season and make it the best ever."

"If the men can be induced to stay on," I said. "How did you manage to collect eighty men? I thought we'd be lucky if we got a dozen from the way they've been showing so much fear of our plantation."

"Some of 'em came from Anse Austin's farm. He didn't need about twenty. They went into town last night and spread the word we were paying two dollars a day. That kind of money quells fears and raises ambition, so we became lucky."

"I'm pleased, Mr. Lindsay. What of the sugar house? Is it in good order?"

"Let's find out," he said, and without another word, he lifted me onto the saddle of his horse and then led the animal through the fields to the long, low brick structure where the machinery and evaporation kettles were kept.

Supported by his arm and my cane, I managed quite well as we moved about the spacious building. I'd been too young to understand much about the process of sugar making before mama and I left for New Orleans ten years ago.

"Things have changed since you were a little girl," Lindsay explained. "We used to run the cane through a grinder that never worked well and left too much juice in the bagasse. That's what's left of the cane after it's squeezed."

"Yes, I remember that," I said. "There used to be mounds of the pressed cane at sugaring time."

"We burn it now, to heat the kettles in which the juice is turned into syrup. And the mill now has three rollers instead of one so we waste no juice. Instead of the old-fashioned kettles, we now use a rolling kind that keeps the syrup moving as the sugar begins to crystallize. We also use hydrometers to tell us exactly when the syrup is ready to be crystallied and how much lime and sulfurous acid to use in clarifying it."

"Everything looks so clean and ready to go," I said. "Mr. Lindsay, you deserve a great deal of credit for this, I know."

"Well, wasn't much else to do with nobody working. The cane grew all by itself practically. We were lucky the

weather stayed right too, and the worms didn't come thi
year. Now we're ready to get back to work. By tomorrow
they'll be stripping the cane and bringing it in. The stack
from the furnaces will be smoking, Miss Carolyn, and it'l
do my heart good to see the place working again."

"Papa will take heart from this," I said. "Mr. Lindsay
what do you know about a woman called Hattie who live
alone somewhere and goes to all the funerals dressed i
white?"

He chuckled. "She's addled, Miss Carolyn. There's nc
other word for it. She's crazy as a loon, but harmless, fa
as I know."

"She seems to take great delight in watching the victim
of that impossible curse being buried."

"That's why we figure she's looney. She even lives in a
shack close by the cemetery so she won't miss anything."

"Do you know where she came from?" I asked.

"Nobody does. She just drifted into town one day abou
. . . oh, twelve or thirteen years ago. She bought a shanty
close by the graveyard and she lives there by herself. Nobody ever comes to see her and she goes no place excep
to buy what provisions she needs. I talked to Rafe Coope
just the other day. He's the mailman in town. He said she
never once got a single piece of mail in all the time she's
been living here. She's a strange one, all right. I guess every
town has got one like that. Nobody pays any attention to
her."

"I'm going to," I said. "The delight she seemed to take
in the funeral of Jeff Horton's father makes me wonder
about her, so I'm going to see her. Today, if my ankle
holds out. I'd like a buggy ready in about an hour, if you
don't mind."

"I'll have it waiting," he promised. "Want to go back
now?"

I nodded. "I'd like to visit with papa for a while. Especially this morning when I have so much to tell him about
the crop and the condition of the sugar house."

I rode Mr. Lindsay's horse sidesaddle back to the house.
Mama was having breakfast when I entered and I talked
to her for a few moments.

"Your father seems some better," she said. "I'm encouraged."

"I'll lighten his day," I told her. "I've just looked over part of the plantation and it's in fine order. Besides, enough men are coming to work to get the crop in. Thanks to Mr. Lindsay."

"He is an efficient and kindly man. Papa is lucky to have him."

I agreed, and when I told papa about my little expedition he was delighted. "I've been lying in this bed for weeks, wondering how the place is doing and afraid it was falling to rot and ruin. Cal Lindsay is only one man, but I guess an exceptional one if he's kept things up with the little help available to him."

"Not only that, papa," I said. "He has eighty men coming to work. That's enough to get the crop in, he says. Of course, they're being paid better than most farms will pay, but Mr. Lindsay says the crop is so good it won't matter much and we can make a profit."

"If I can only get up and be about," papa complained. "Whenever I try to take more than twenty steps or so, my knees cave in and I'm apt to fall down."

"Which reminds me, papa, it's time for your medicine. Seems to me Dr. Shea's nostrums are doing you some good. You're much better than when mama and I arrived."

"Well, some better," he acknowledge with a wan smile. "I sure am not myself, though."

I was tempted to bring up the subject of the ship's bell and the whistle, but I refrained because it might upset him to even recall them. Papa needed all the rest and peace of mind he could get. We talked about the arpents of standing cane, the weather, and drifted back into the time when the packet rode through the crevasse and all this trouble began.

"The water stood five feet high in the fields," papa said. "We were wiped out far as the crop was concerned. So was everybody else. Anse Austin was hit very hard. Even his sugar house was washed away and all his machinery destroyed. He weathered it, but not easily. He's still paying off on his losses today."

"Do you know what I'd like to do, papa? I'd like t sprinkle oil all around that old hulk and set it afire. I stands there reminding everybody of something they' rather forget."

"I thought of that many times, but the temper of th town makes it impossible, Carolyn. Those who believe i the curse and in ghostly presences claim things will ge worse if we destroy the packet where the ghosts are sup posed to live. I know it sounds like crazy talk, but that how they feel and we have trouble enough getting folks t work for us now. I wouldn't take the chance if I were you."

"You know best, papa. But this plantation is going t be running again. I can promise you that, and when you'r up and about once more, things will get back to norma quickly."

I thought he might have commented in a discourage fashion, for I knew he doubted he would ever recover, bu papa was not a weak man, nor one to give up easily.

"I hope that day comes soon. I feel that I'm taking yo away from New Orleans and what could be the most im portant few years of your life. On the plantation there' nothing but work, no young beaux coming to call. . . ."

"Papa," I said with a smile, "Dr. Shea doesn't come only to see you."

"Oh, I noticed that. Jeff Horton is courting you too, I'm sure."

"Randy Austin is also interested. That makes three and no girl could handle any more than that, papa."

"Nonsense. In New Orleans there'd be thirty."

"Yes," I agreed, "but they'd not be of a cut equal to that of any of these three, papa."

"Do you favor any one of them?" he asked.

"I'm not sure. I think so, but I haven't been here long enough to make up my mind."

"It would be Jeff Horton," he said with the wisdom of his years, enabling him to guess that accurately. "He's a fine young man. But then, so are the others, though Randy seems a trifle young—"

"Papa, I haven't decided."

"I know, my dear. You've too much on your mind."

If he ever knew how much, I was afraid he might some-how get out of bed despite his illness. I hated keeping things from him, but under the circumstances there seemed no other way to handle this problem. He would be able to do little to help and he'd only grow weaker because of his efforts to do something.

I urged him to rest and promised I'd be in to see him in the afternoon. I gave him no explanation of what I intended to do with my time until then. Mr. Lindsay had the buggy waiting outside the front door and I drove to the village, through it and on toward the cemetery. I thought I had seen the shack in which Hattie, the woman in white, lived her solitary existence, and Mr. Lindsay had confirmed that she lived near the graveyard.

It looked more run down than it really was, I noted upon getting closer to it. I left the buggy and, using my cane, I made my way down a short path to the door. The structure was more in need of paint than anything else, for it looked quite sturdy and weatherproof to me now.

I raised my hand to knock when the window to the left of the door was suddenly raised and I was taken aback by the sight of a rifle barrel pointed straight at me.

"Hattie," I said, "there's no need for a gun. I'm only paying you a visit. To talk."

"Don't want to talk. Go away. You're one of them. I want nothing to do with you. Go away or I swear I'll shoot."

"What are you afraid of?" I asked. "I'm quite harmless. Please stop pointing the gun at me."

"In one minute I'll shoot," she threatened in a strident, highly excited voice. At the same time I heard the hammer of the rifle click back. Even if she was bluffing and had no intention of shooting, to be faced with a gun ready to go off by even slight pressure on the trigger was enough to unnerve me. I backed away from the door.

"Very well," I said. "You're making a mistake, but if it is your desire never to speak to anyone, I won't insist on seeing you. But I am disappointed, Hattie."

I turned around and limped away, my back toward the rifle, and every step was filled with anxiety, for I knew she was an unstable woman and that rifle was so ready for firing. It occurred to me also that I'd never even seen her, for she'd been hiding behind the window curtains. I felt safe only after I climbed into the buggy, and I was now convinced that Hattie was a madwoman, highly dangerous and unpredictable. I didn't intend to make the mistake of trying to talk to her again. Not when she had a rifle.

I did stop in the village to buy a few things I needed. I was treated politely, but not with any degree of warmth. I represented those who fell under the captain's curse and therefore I was to be more feared than accepted.

I emerged from the general store with my free arm laden with a large bag and my right hand using the cane, and managed to descend the wooden stairs and walk toward my buggy. At the moment when I was about to place the bag of supplies in the buggy I heard a wild scream behind me. I turned quickly and saw a man running down the middle of the dusty street.

He was tall, and thin to the point of emaciation. He had a full beard, dirty and stained. His white hair was an unruly mop which looked as if it hadn't been combed in a decade. He wore a faded shirt and overalls. His feet were bare.

He kept screaming. It sounded to me as if he was shouting for help, but, incongruously, the score of people either on the sidewalks or in their yards scarcely looked up. It was as if they didn't even hear him, or see him, and that thought gave me cold shivers.

He noticed me too and came to an abrupt halt in his mad running. He now began walking toward me, and there was a malevolent gleam in his eyes as he stared straight at me, and his scarred face made him look uglier than ever. I backed up until my spine was pressed against the buggy. Still he kept on, slowly now, until he was very close to me.

"Ye're his daughter," he said. "I hear he's sick and dying and that makes me glad. It'll be your turn next."

"Who are you?" I asked. "Why do you dare to address me this way?"

He opened his mouth to give a loud howl of laughter

while he slapped his thigh hard and doubled up in this strange mirth.

"I'll tell you who I am. My son, everybody I loved, is dead because your father and those like him wouldn't throw us a rope or try to reach us."

I said, "You're one of those who escaped from the burning packet? You should be bowing your head in gratitude that your life was spared."

"The life of my Anne and my son and daughter, they were not spared. It needed only a rope or a hand, any small thing, to save them. But your pa and the others just stood there and watched everybody die. I was a successful man before that happened and I lost everything. I keep reliving that night over and over. I keep thinking I'm still on the deck of that damned boat. Every day I feel that I'm dying over again. And your pa is to blame. He'll die. Oh yes, he'll die just like the rest of them and there'll be no lifting of that curse until the last one is dead."

"I don't know your name, sir," I said. "but I feel sorry for you. Sorry that you lost those you loved, but even more sorry for your twisted mind and your suffering. However, I do not admire your wild and foolish talk, sir. Good day."

I climbed aboard the buggy. The man stood there, making no attempt to interfere and saying nothing more. That haunted look in his eyes was the most discomforting thing I'd ever seen. I was afraid of this man. I disliked him for what he said and while I honestly felt much sympathy for him, I was going to stay away from him if that was possible.

I noted that the street was now well populated with villagers who had emerged from their homes and the stores to watch the drama unfold. I suppose they were disappointed that there'd been no violence. I picked up the reins and drove away, fearful the man would try to stop me or attempt to board the buggy. He made no move whatever, though, not even when the dust from the buggy wheels and the horse's hooves enveloped him in a thick, reddish cloud.

I thanked whatever guardian angel watched over me.

The episode could have been far more dangerous. I knew the man was Edward Baker. His deeply scarred face identified him beyond any doubt. While he had not actually harmed me, I believed his actions sufficiently threatening that someone should know about them. I drove directly to Dr. Shea's home and office. Unfortunately, he wasn't there, though a woman in the waiting room said he was expected any moment. I decided not to wait. He'd be up to see papa soon anyway and I could ask him then.

I might have gone to tell Jeff Horton about it, but I didn't even know where he lived or if he maintained a business office here, nor was I about to ask anyone. I'd had enough adventures for one afternoon. I was glad to begin my drive back to the plantation.

As I neared the spot where my horse had bolted, I repressed a shudder and was inclined to urge the horse to greater speed, but I refused to allow myself to panic just because this was where I'd almost been either badly injured or killed. I was fortunate to have escaped with only a sprained ankle.

I was still fighting the urge to get away from this spot when I heard the crack of a rifle and the whine of a bullet that must have passed very close to me, without hitting the buggy or anything else. There was no doubt this was a second attempt on my life. I half-arose from the seat, slapped the reins hard and the horse took off at top speed while I braced myself in case of more shooting. I didn't relax until I was a mile away from the scene, and then I allowed the horse to resume a casual pace while I sat shivering visibly.

It came to me that the man who accosted me in the village had actually threatened my life. Or, at least, predicted that I too would die along with the victims of the curse.

After I'd left him I'd stopped at Dr. Shea's and then I'd proceeded at a leisurely pace for home. By taking short cuts through fields, anyone in the village could have reached the scene of the shooting in time to waylay me. I made up my mind not to venture out alone again if I could possibly avoid it. I began to realize that the curse imposed upon the fathers must carry through to their children. Jeff might even now be in peril, because his father had just died and he could be next.

At that moment, shaken by my ordeal, my mind full of conflicting thoughts and fears, I suddenly realized that I was in love with Jeff. Thinking that he might be in danger brought home that feeling. Nothing except real love could have inspired such awful anxiety in me.

Now my mind whirled even faster than it had before. I decided not to say anything at the plantation about this latest attempt. There was no way I could prove it and there was always the chance papa might inadvertently hear about it. I wanted to avoid worrying him at any cost. I would tell Jeff and Dr. Shea because I knew they'd never talk about it. Someone should know in the event that this were tried again. Next time the would-be murderer might be successful.

I brought the horse to a faster pace. I didn't want to be alone. Not now, when I could still fancy I heard the whine of the bullet and the crack of the rifle. If only I knew what, or who, was responsible. I hadn't the faintest idea, but my belief in the power of a dead man's curse was not growing any stronger. More and more it seemed as though the curse had something behind it. Supernatural or human, whoever planned these two attempts on my life was very likely to try again.

I was never so happy as when I pulled up in front of the mansion. I left the horse tied up there. Mr. Lindsay was apparently in the fields, or the sugar house, for I saw no sign of him.

I took as firm control over my nerves as I could and limped into the house, carrying the bag of supplies and even now steeled against the idea of a bullet being fired into my back by some mad killer who had followed me home.

EIGHT

That night, to add to my worries, papa grew worse and we had to send for Dr. Shea. He gave us little to hope for, and that night I waited in terror for the sound of the ship's bell and the screech of the whistle. Papa, of course, knew nothing of what had happened to me, from my reception by Hattie to my mad confrontation with Ed Baker and, finally, the shot taken at me with murderous intent.

"It is my belief that he has been too well buoyed up with hope that the plantation is about to get going again," Dr. Shea said. "My advice would be to tell him as little as possible. Oh, let him think about it and let him hope, but not to so great an extent."

"We can't keep him from knowing that eighty men are coming to work, nor can we prevent the sound of the sugar house in operation from reaching him, Doctor."

"Yes, I realize that, Carolyn," he agreed. "But don't get him to a pitch where he wants to get out of bed and join those eighty men at work. When he discovers he cannot do so, the shock could be bad for him."

"We'll do our best," I said. "Thank you anyway."

He took my hand and held it a long time. "I wish I could come here to see you and not have all this sorrow and worry around you. There are so many things we could do together. There are dances, and some of the bigger plantations give elaborate balls. I'm always invited and I rarely go because I have no one I care enough about to go with. It's different now. I'd be proud to take you anywhere. And very, very happy, Carolyn."

"Thank you again," I said. "I too wish this was not a house of anguish. Tell me, quite frankly, is there any hope for my father?"

"There is always hope," he said. "In this case, though, it's quite forlorn, I'm afraid. I don't even know what ails him. No more than I did with any of the others. They simply get sick, wither and die, and nothing I can do stops the progress of the sickness. I am unable to properly treat such people because it is impossible to treat an unknown illness."

"I understand," I said. "Papa will soon die, then?"

"I cannot stem the disease," he admitted.

"It will break my heart if papa dies, but if it is unavoidable then I hope it will be the last of these deaths."

Dr. Shea shook his head in sorrow. "I cannot believe that, after what has happened. There will be someone else, for there are still several others who fall under that curse."

"It is my belief," I said, "that this so-called curse is no more than a fallacy and some human, satanic mind is behind these deaths, taking advantage of the ravings of that captain and the superstitions of the villagers."

"My dear Carolyn, how often I have told myself the same thing. Then another grows ill as one more dies. It seems that since only one is deathly ill at a time, the terror lasts longer, which I think is deliberate."

"You do not still believe there is a human element behind this?"

"A number of people have died, Carolyn, and I cannot account for their deaths. I have sent samples of their blood and the contents of their stomachs to Baton Rouge for study and the reports came back that there is nothing wrong. These people die of no known ailment and they show no symptoms except extreme fatigue, which finally results in their deaths."

"Papa is the only one now affected?"

"So far as I know. I too hope he will be the last but, believe me, I am doing everything in my power to keep him alive."

"I'm sure you are and for a little while he seemed some better. Now, if there is a human element behind this, it is murder, Doctor. Nothing less, but without any known reason."

"Yes, I agree. As you say, there is no motive. Your father and all the other victims were well-respected, honest, hard-working men, and some were quite successful. Some made only a moderate living. No discrimination is shown on that point."

"Today," I explained, "I went to the little cabin where a woman named Hattie lives. I saw her at the funeral for Jeff's father. She was dressed in white, she seemed to take great delight in watching the services and I wanted to find out why this could be. When I reached her cabin she thrust a rifle out of a window and aimed it at me with a threat that she'd shoot if I didn't go away at once."

"I wish you had told me your intentions," Dr. Shea said. "Hattie is a deranged woman. Not so mad that she must be locked up, but addled enough to make such threats. I don't know that she'd carry them out, but guns have been known to go off accidentally in the hands of nervous and distraught people. Please don't try to see her again. At least not as long as she is close by a gun."

"Who is she, Doctor? Why does she act this way?"

"Nobody knows. She offers no explanation. Where she came from, or why she picked this town to settle in is a mystery."

"Have you ever treated her?"

"Not treated her, no. But I did talk to her. There was some thought of having her put away and it became necessary that I see her. She wouldn't let me in at first, but when I told her the next visitor would be the sheriff, she gave in."

"She is mad," I said. "After today I'm not sure but that she should be locked up."

"I have to disagree. She threatened you. Yes, of course she did, but she's a highly nervous woman. Yet I would swear she'd never have fired the gun."

"If you'd seen it pointed at you——" I began.

"I know. I don't blame you for being afraid of her.

However, I do not feel she is mad enough to be taken into custody. Her little cabin is neat and she herself is careful of her grooming and dresses well. A bit old-fashioned perhaps, but she hasn't bought anything in all the years she has been here."

"What of a man named Edward Baker? He is an unkempt person and a man of violence. I have met him."

"He would behave angrily toward you," Dr. Shea admitted. "He is one of two survivors of the wreck and has bestowed his individual curse on all those who stood by while the packet burned."

"Then does he not have a firm reason for wanting to kill all these people?"

"Indeed he has, and don't think he wasn't suspected. However, he drinks too much. There is some small income he receives each month, I think from insurance policies on his kin who died in the wreck. With this money he becomes very intoxicated and is often locked up. In almost all of the deaths, when the whistle blew, Ed Baker was accounted for, either dead drunk and in the lockup, or drinking with a few cronies who stand him because he does have a little money. He was absolved of all suspicion long ago. We cannot accuse him, Carolyn."

"And Willie Spencer? I have not met him yet but if he is like Hattie and Baker I certainly do not care to."

"Well, he's quite harmless. A strange man, I admit. I don't know what sort of person he was before the wreck. His kin—all of them—died in the fire. Willie mourned them and buried them and then went into seclusion. Like Hattie, he has an isolated cabin about a mile out of town, not far from the road you take on the way back."

"Doctor," I exclaimed. "Two attempts were made to kill me along that road."

"There was another besides the one where you sprained your ankle?"

"I'm certain someone took a shot at me today. I'd left the village and was on my way back."

Dr. Shea suddenly stepped close to my chair and bent down over me. He placed his hands on my shoulders and his expression was most serious.

"I'm concerned about you, Carolyn. Very much so be cause I'm falling in love with you."

"Please," I begged him, "I'm flattered but this is n time to ask me to even think about being in love."

"I know. I'm aware of that and I will not press it. only wanted you to know why I am so concerned. An when the time comes when you need help, I hope you wi call upon me first."

I knew exactly what he meant. "Papa is going to die isn't he?"

"Yes," Dr. Shea said gruffly, as if he didn't want t utter that one word.

I bowed my head and Dr. Shea resumed his chair acros from me. "I've known it all the time, of course," I said "I was hoping, but I know how forlorn that hope is. No one of the men so afflicted have lived. All of their death were to the tolling of the ship's bell and the sound of it whistle."

"There were no exceptions," he admitted. "I couldn' be so cruel as to try and deceive you any longer."

"How long?" I asked. I raised my head to look directl at him.

"I can't be sure. It may be very soon; it may be a wee or two. As I don't know what causes him to be ill, I can not predict accurately. But it will be soon, I'm afraid."

"He must not know. Neither must mama."

"Trust me, Carolyn."

"I do. With all my heart."

He arose. "I have to go now. Please don't go nea Hattie, and if Ed Baker annoys you let me know and I' see to it he never does again."

"Do you recommend that I do not visit Mr. Spencer?"

"Willie will do you no harm. He's an educated man. H doesn't seem bitter like Ed Baker, and he has devoted hi life to the study of many things: religions all over th world, languages, science. While he does not show himsel too often, he is nonetheless well liked."

I picked up my cane to accompany Dr. Shea to th door. He gently took the cane away from me. "Try i without assistance," he said. "If the ankle pains too much by all means go back to the cane, but I want you to get better as quickly as you can. It seems your life is in danger and if you depend on the cane all the time, you may not be able to move about quickly enough."

I took a few steps and the ankle supported me well, though pain did shoot up my leg and Dr. Shea had to take my arm. At the door he handed me the cane.

"Another day or two, I'm afraid. Tomorrow I'll change the bandage. Good afternoon, Carolyn. Please don't fail to call on me if there is anything I can do to help. I'll be back in the morning to see your father."

I stayed in the doorway until he drove off in his buggy. Then I hobbled into the kitchen, where Yvonne was busy preparing the evening meal.

"I wish we could find a cook," I said to her. "This should not be among your duties."

"We have to eat," she said with a smile. "Cooks are hard to come by in this house. They come and they go. Most are bad, anyway."

"At least you remain," I said. "I'm grateful for that."

"I have been here too long to leave now." She dipped a ladle into a savory stew and handed me a small portion of it. "There is ginger in it," she explained. "I do not feel it will be harmful to your father."

I tasted of the deliciously smelling and tasting concoction of meat, vegetables and spices. "It's wonderful. I can't see how it will harm him."

She said, "He will soon die, Miss Carolyn. I think you know that."

"Yes," I said. "I do, but how do you know?"

"I have seen men die before. I have watched this sickness come over others in the village and they all die in the same way. I am truly sorry, *mademoiselle,* but if there is no help for it, may it come without pain."

"Thank you, Yvonne. You have been with papa so many years that you must know the Austin family quite well. Is Anse Austin a covetous man?"

"When it comes to taking over this plantation, *mademoiselle,* he would do almost anything to get it. He is an ambitious man and he has always wanted to add your

father's farm to his. In the flood, when the packet was
wrecked, he lost most everything he owned, but he has
managed to get through that and he is doing well now. As
I've said, he is ambitious and he prizes this farm."

"Enough to kill a man to get it?" I asked.

"Perhaps. But it is not Anse Austin who kills your
papa. It is the curse. Anse had nothing to do with the
deaths of all the others, so why should he try to kill your
father?"

"By using the deaths of all the others to hide the fact
that papa's death may be different."

"Why different? I tell you it is the curse that kills him,
mademoiselle. Only the curse. Anse will be lucky if he
does not find himself next."

"He has been ailing," I admitted.

"It may not be my privilege to say this, *mademoiselle....*"

"Yvonne, you are as much a member of this family as I.
You have the right to say anything."

"Merci. It has been true so far as it concerns your papa,
but I was not so sure of you or your mama. So I will say
it. Do not encourage the Austin young man."

"Randolph?"

"Oui. I have seen him in angry moods, and he is easily
capable of killing a man. He is most jealous and will resent the way Dr. Shea calls upon you. As well as Jeff
Horton."

"He's so young," I said.

"He is sixteen and a half, but big for his age. It is too
bad his brain is not as perfect as his body." She began
stirring the stew again. "I must see to my work."

I left her, impressed with her knowledge of what went
on and accepting her warning against Randy Austin. I
didn't especially care for that young man anyway.

I was not too concerned with clothes these days, but
both Jeff and Dr. Shea were calling this evening, so I
changed from the rather plain, unadorned dress I'd been
wearing because it was practical on a plantation like this.
My somewhat limited wardrobe provided me with a pink
jersey, so tightly laced at the waist that I needed mama's

help to draw the laces and adjust the Langtry bustle, the new type of bustle which worked on a pivot and could be raised when I wished to sit down. Upon arising it instantly sprang back into its proper position and was far less tiring to wear than the ordinary kind.

"Are you growing serious over any of these young men?" mama asked as she tugged at the laces.

"Not yet," I replied with a gasp, for the breath was being forced out of my lungs as the laces tightened.

"Dressing up this way, I thought perhaps you were."

"There's no time for that," I said.

"With your father as ill as he is, I didn't think you'd spend your days frivolously."

"I'm spending my time in trying to get the plantation going and in doing what I can to find out what's going on here that causes men to die so mysteriously."

"I fear greatly for your father, my dear. He seems to grow weaker and weaker. When I last saw him, he was barely able to talk and all he wanted to do was sleep. Dr. Shea is concerned as well."

"So long as he breathes, I will not give up. Nor even after that, for others are bound to grow ill too."

Mama sat down to rest after her exertions, while I pulled on my gown and adjusted it before the mirror.

"What will we do, Carolyn, when it's over? You see, I have no hope. One must be practical even in the face of such sorrow."

"I don't know, mama, except that I shall stay right here. I will not let the plantation go. Not even to Anse Austin."

"I'm sure he would offer a great price."

"I have no doubt of it. Unless you order me to sell the farm. . . ."

"Oh no, Carolyn. I would order you to do nothing of the sort. For myself, I could not handle this. You are young and full of energy. There will be money enough to see it through, but even if you asked me to, I'd be unable to help."

"Mama, I refuse to make any plans while papa is alive. Time enough for that afterwards. If there is an afterwards, because papa is a fighter and he won't give up easily.

People have been known to recover from serious illnesses before."

"This is not an illness," mama said slowly. "It is a curse placed upon him by a man who was mad as he shouted at us. Nobody could have helped rescue anyone. It would have only been the sacrifice of more lives if any of us had tried to swim out. You have no idea how awful that night was."

Before I could remark on that, we heard a carriage being driven up to the door. Mama hurried to a window and looked out.

"It's Randolph Austin," she said.

"Oh, drat it," I complained irritably. "Jeff is coming tonight too."

"Dr. Shea said he would look in after dark," mama added. "It looks as if you're going to have your hands full this evening, dear. That's as it should be, even in times of sadness."

"Do I look all right?" I asked.

"You're beautiful. Absolutely beautiful."

"Should I stop in to see papa?"

"He's asleep. I wouldn't disturb him now. I'd like him to see you in that dress. You're so grown up in it. Perhaps later when he's awake, you can visit."

"I'll be sure to. Will you come down to supper?"

"No, I have to stay with him. Ask Yvonne to bring me a tray. Carolyn, what do you think of that woman?"

"Yvonne? I like her. Besides, she's very competent and she adores papa."

"Yes," mama said, "I noticed that from the first. However, I do trust her."

"I know. I do too, mama. I'd better go down now and keep Randy company. He isn't going to like it when two other men turn up tonight."

Randy jumped to his feet as I entered the drawing room. Unlike Jeff and Dr. Shea, he was not given to social amenities and, as a result, he was shy and sometimes clumsy. I felt sorry for him because he was trying so hard, but I could never come to like this young man to any great extent, for I could almost sense a strain of cruelty in him.

"Evenin,' Miss Carolyn," he said. "Guess I came too early, didn't I?"

Not if you were asked to supper, I thought. Which he hadn't been. "I'm delighted to see you, Randolph." I gave him my hand. "I hope you will do me the honor of taking supper with me. Otherwise I must eat alone."

"Well now, we had kind of a late dinner, but I'd be glad to keep you company. You're pretty."

"Thank you," I said, and I took his arm as we walked to the dining room. Yvonne, who missed nothing, already had a second plate set. Randy and I dined mostly in silence. When I began a conversation it ended abruptly, for Randy never carried through on any subject. We had just finished one of Yvonne's wonderful floating island puddings when we heard Jeff ride up on horseback. I will confess that I forgot about Randy as I hurried to meet Jeff at the door.

I gave him both my hands as I pulled him into the reception hall. "I am glad to see you, Jeff," I said.

"I take that as the greatest compliment of my lifetime," he smiled. He looked over my shoulder. "Good evening, Randy. How are your folks?"

"All right, I guess. Pa's been ailin'."

I looked around. Randy was scowling and not trying to hide his displeasure over Jeff's arrival.

"Come along, Randy," I said, and I led them into the drawing room, where Yvonne appeared with brandy for Jeff and a look at Randy which told him as well as if she'd spoken that he was too young for alcoholic beverages.

"How is your father?" Jeff asked me.

"I haven't seen him since early afternoon. Mama said he was sleeping mostly. She's worried about him and so am I. Dr. Shea is not optimistic."

"Dr. Shea is also helpless to do anything for these people," Jeff said. "Will he come out tonight?"

"Yes. He will likely be here before long."

"He's comin' too?" Randy asked in fresh dismay.

"Yes, Randy. To see papa."

Randy lapsed into silence that was almost sullen. I was

embarrassed by his attitude, but Jeff seemed to be amused by it. Jeff and I talked about the plantation and our plans for it. This interested Randy, though he had no comments to make. About half an hour later, right after dark, Dr. Shea drove up in his buggy. I went out to greet him.

He shook hands with Jeff and nodded casually to Randy. It was clear that he didn't care for that young man, and Randy still kept scowling.

"I'll run up and see how your father is," Dr. Shea said. Halfway up the stairs he paused and looked down. "I won't be long. Good night, Randy. Good night, Jeff."

" 'Good night'?" Randy looked puzzled. Then he made a wry face. "What makes him think I'm leavin'?"

"It's only his hope and wish," Jeff said. "Sit down, Randy. I hear your pa's ailing."

"Yep, he is. Kinda drags around and leaves all the hard work for me."

"You're big and strong," Jeff said.

"If we had this plantation too," Randy announced with surprising candor, "we'd have so many hands workin' for us I wouldn't have to do more'n tell 'em what to do."

"Which reminds me, Carolyn," Jeff said. "There's talk all over the village that you and Cal Lindsay are hiring and the plantation will be running again soon."

"That's right," I said. "I do hope some of the villagers will come to work for us."

"I have an idea some will. Enough of them too, what with the men Randy's father is sending over. You ought to get in a good crop by the looks of the cane. I checked around the fields yesterday."

"I hope we can get it all in. A rainstorm now would ruin the crop."

"Ain't been no rain in more'n a month," Randy said. "Won't be the rain that'll ruin it, but the sun."

Dr. Shea came downstairs and looked at Randy as if he wondered why he was still there.

"Your father's not doing well," he told me. "I'm sorry to say so, but there's been a change today."

"Is he awake?" I asked.

"No. He woke up somewhat when I was there and took

his medicine before he went back to sleep. I'll stay awhile if you don't mind, Miss Carolyn."

"I'm grateful you will, Doctor," I said formally, mostly for Randy's sake. He was sulking enough now and if he got it into his head that Dr. Shea's call was not entirely a professional one, he might resent that even more.

The conversation was a bit strained. Dr. Shea talked about papa's condition, Jeff about his New Orleans office, which, I judged, did a substantial business. Randy had nothing to say.

I was actually becoming embarrassed at the long silences when someone rode up on horseback, and in a hurry, from the approach of the horse.

Yvonne went to the door and hurried back into the drawing room. "It's your pa, Randy," she said. "He's taken mighty sick and your ma wants you home now."

"I'll go along," Dr. Shea said. "Lucky I was here. Come on, Randy. I suspect your father's inflamed stomach is acting up again."

The messenger rode off, followed by Dr. Shea's buggy and then by the carriage Randy was driving. Jeff looked more worried than pleased at their abrupt departure.

"I hope that's all the matter with Anse," he said. "I've been wondering for days when somebody else would get sick from that ailment Dr. Shea can't diagnose."

I felt a sudden wave of apprehension and nervousness. "If someone gets sick, then . . . then papa is going to die. That's the way it works all the time, doesn't it?"

Jeff nodded. "I'm afraid so, Carolyn. Seems to me time is running out. I hate to say that, but we have to look at this with a hard eye."

"I know, Jeff."

"More and more I've been thinking that maybe it's not the vengeance of the packet captain that makes your father sick. If somebody wanted his plantation bad enough he could be doing something to see your pa's not getting well."

"Jeff," I cried out, aghast at the idea, "you don't mean Dr. Shea?"

"Oh no . . . no, not at all. I'm thinking more of Anse

and Randy. The way they're after the farm is pitiful. Soon as your father got sick they began talking about it."

"I noticed that Randy mentioned it tonight," I said. "Oh, Jeff, I can't see how they could be scheming to kill papa."

"If he is being slowly murdered, there has to be a reason for it and Anse has got the only one that makes any sense. Doc Shea has no interest in anything but medicine, and especially none in running a sugar plantation. It has to be Anse."

"To make papa so ill it would have to be done with poison? Dr. Shea would surely have detected that before now. Besides, he seems to be suffering from exactly the same malady that killed all the others, so it must all be part of a ghastly scheme."

Jeff nodded. "I guess I'm a little crazy to talk that way. It's because I keep thinking so much about it. My father died a couple of days ago and I want to get to the bottom of that too, because he was as healthy and hard working as your pa used to be. For two men like that to get sick with what seems to be the same disease and wither and die in such a short time is all but impossible under normal conditions. Most of the others who died were healthy too, just before they were brought down by this strange sickness."

"No wonder everybody thinks they died from a dead man's curse," I said sadly. "I almost believe it myself."

We talked about the other victims, trying to establish some thread besides the curse that would link them all. We found no answers. An hour must have gone by before Dr. Shea returned, driving his buggy fast.

"Anse has come down with it," he said. "The same illness. It's not his stomach inflammation this time. He's getting weaker by the hour."

I arose slowly. "Doctor, when a second man comes down with the illness, the first sick man usually dies. Is that right?"

Dr. Shea only nodded once before he rushed upstairs. Jeff and I followed him. In the sick room papa lay quietly, his chest barely raising and lowering the sheet that covered him. His face was gray and it was not hard to see that the end would come soon. Mama was quietly weeping. I held her in my arms for a moment before I led her out of the room. When I returned, Jeff met me in the corridor.

"Doctor Shea thinks it's best that you wait downstairs."

We waited until dawn and still papa clung to life. Dr. Shea, red eyed from lack of sleep, refused to go to the village and rested on one of the sofas in the drawing room. I covered him with a blanket. Jeff and I walked out into the gray dawn. We didn't talk. Words seemed so inconsequential at the moment.

NINE

Papa was still fighting all the next day, though there was no hope according to Dr. Shea. Papa had a strong, durable heart and it refused to stop. Mama had been given a sleeping draught so she might get some rest, but I only dozed from time to time. I had changed out of my frilly gown and into the more practical type of dress I wore around the plantation. Jeff went home after our brief walk in the dawn. Dr. Shea found it necessary to go to the village for his office hours and a few calls he had to make.

I sat beside papa's bed, holding his hand, watching his slow breathing. He seemed to be in no pain, for which I was grateful. I had already prepared myself mentally for what was going to happen. Still, papa held on. I ate something for dinner and had a few bites at supper. Dr. Shea came twice, shook his head and went back to his other patients. Jeff came early in the evening and stayed until almost midnight.

"How long can this go on?" I exclaimed as he took his

leave. "Papa isn't going to get well. I know that. I don't want him to die, but I don't want him hanging on like this either. I don't think he's in pain. . . ."

"It's obvious he's not." Jeff tried to comfort me. "Please try to get some rest, Carolyn. I'll stay with him. You can't keep going like this without breaking down."

He was right and I knew it. "Thank you, darling Jeff. If you will stay with him . . . and call me. . . ."

He nodded. "Rest now. You're doing him no good by staying awake and risking your own health."

I nodded. "He'd be the first one to order me to go to bed. Thank you again, Jeff. Without you I'd be lost."

I went to mama's room and looked in. She was fast asleep under the influence of Dr. Shea's draught. In my own room I didn't undress. I pulled down the bed covers and lay down with the idea that if it was necessary for me to awaken quickly I'd lose no time getting to papa's side. I closed my eyes and fell asleep in a matter of a few seconds.

I never did know if it was the bell or the whistle that brought me out of my sleep. I sat up, dimly aware of where I was and what was going on. The bell aboard the ship was clanging and the whistle was booming a sound to be heard for miles.

My bedroom door burst open and Jeff came in. "It's happened," he said. "I'm going to the wreck and see if I can find anything."

"I'm going too," I said. "Don't try to stop me."

"All right. Yvonne is awake. She can stay with your father. Hurry! Maybe we can catch whoever is responsible for all that noise."

"And all these murders," I added. "How is papa?"

"Just the same."

"Then the whistle is wrong. He isn't dead."

"Some died soon after the whistle sounded," Jeff told me. "Don't get up any hope."

I tied the laces on my shoes, threw a wrap over my shoulders and followed Jeff down the stairs. Yvonne was seated beside papa's bed, I noted on my way out.

Jeff took my hand and we ran across the wide expanse

of the grounds around the mansion. We came to the path that led us in the direction of the wreck. The bell and the whistle had long since ceased making their lethal noises and the night seemed unduly quiet and dark. Had Jeff not been with me it would have taken me twice as long to reach the wreck.

We scrambled up the incline to the knoll. Neither of us had been thoughtful enough to bring a lantern so we were badly handicapped, but we got aboard and we explored the decks and the cabins. We found no trace of anyone—nothing whatsoever. Yet the bell had clanged and the whistle had blown, both sounds carried by the wind so that everybody within two or three miles must have heard their ominous sound.

"There is nothing here," Jeff said.

"The whistle blew and we heard the bell. There must have been someone to create those sounds," I said.

"Yes, of course. But who and, just as important, how? Believe me, the whistle didn't blow and the bell wasn't rung. Not by the rope attached to it."

"We should have brought lanterns," I said.

"That was my fault. I was in too much of a hurry. We'd best come back by daylight and look for tracks or any signs of someone's having been on board."

"Take me back, Jeff," I begged. "We were crazy to come here at night anyway. I want to be with papa."

He took my hand again and led me off the packet. As we crossed the creaky, sagging gangplank, Jeff told me he just had an idea.

"I'll explain it later. We can't put it to work now anyway. I'll tell you about it when the right time comes."

We hurried through the night, staying on the path, and by the time we came into view of the plantation, we were running. We both saw Dr. Shea's buggy outside and every ground-floor window was illuminated by candle and lamplight. Upstairs, where papa lay dying, his window was only dimly lit. I had a premonition of what that meant.

Dr. Shea was in the drawing room with mama and Yvonne. Mama wept openly and loudly while Yvonne only lowered her head, but I sensed that her grief was as intense as mama's. I looked at Dr. Shea and he nodded somberly. Papa was dead.

"I'm glad you're here, Jeff," Dr. Shea said. "I've got to see Anse Austin. Word came he's worse."

"You go along," Jeff said. "I'll stay here and do what's to be done."

I had presence of mind enough to reach Dr. Shea before he was at the door. "Thank you, Doctor, for being here. I know how pressed you have been."

"Dear Carolyn," he said, "I wish I could have done more. I feel guilty that my knowledge is not sufficient to stop these deaths, or even explain them."

"I should have been with him," I said.

"To what purpose? He was unconscious and knew nothing of what was going on or who was at his side. Yvonne sent Cal Lindsay for me when she thought your father was slipping fast."

"Jeff and I went to the wreck," I explained. "We hoped to find someone there who caused the whistle to sound and the bell to ring. Of course we found no one."

"At least you tried, and that's what your father would have done too. I'll be back in the morning."

I nodded wordlessly and closed the door after he left. I returned to the drawing room and sat down. Mama came to my side, sharing the sofa. I held her in my arms and comforted her as best I knew how. Jeff sent Yvonne for Cal Lindsay and he appeared so quickly he must have been right outside the house. Jeff and Cal talked for a few moments and soon afterward I heard Cal riding to the village. Jeff was taking charge of whatever had to be done and I was grateful to him.

When he and Yvonne rejoined us, I dried my tears and composed myself. "Mama, we have things to discuss."

She looked up, puzzled for a moment, and then she nodded. "Yes . . . I want him buried in the village cemetery. He was a religious man so there must be a church service."

"I'll tend to it," Jeff offered.

"Thank you," mama said. "I'm all right now. I knew this was coming and there was no way to stop it. I

houldn't have broken down as I did. I'm going to say
his now, so you'll be forewarned, Carolyn. When the
uneral is over I am not coming back to this house or this
plantation. I don't care what is done with them. Burn them
oth if you like. They have blighted my life and killed my
usband. Yvonne, I hope you will be kind enough to assist
ne with preparing my baggage."

"*Oui, madame,*" Yvonne said. "I think you are wise to
ave." She turned to me. "What about you, *made-
oiselle?*"

"I'm not leaving," I said. "I won't even consider it until
know who and what killed papa and more than a dozen
thers. I also intend, with Cal Lindsay's help, to get this
lantation going again and become as profitable as it once
vas. I cannot allow papa's years of work and planning to
ade away."

"Whatever you wish," mama said. "I do think it unwise
f you to try to contend with the mystery that rules the
lantation and the village. All this talk of a curse might
e true. I laughed at the idea once but I don't laugh any
nore. Stay if you must, and I admire you for your cour-
ge, but I could not bear it after your father's death."

"Very well, mama," I said. "I'm not afraid and I have
nany friends who will help to look out for me. Now, I
hink you'd better lie down. I'll stay with you. Jeff, will
ou and Yvonne remain to meet those whom Dr. Shea
vill send out?"

They agreed and I led mama upstairs. The door to
apa's room was closed and I escorted her past it swiftly
efore she could decide she wished to go inside. Mama
vas existing solely on willpower now. It wouldn't take
nuch to make her grow ill and weak. That must not hap-
en.

I gave her another of Dr. Shea's powders, shaking the
ontents of the little white packet into half a glass of
vater. Mama took it without an argument, which was
roof of how close she was to breaking down. I didn't
now where I got the courage to keep going.

I sat with mama for more than an hour before she
nally fell asleep. During that time I heard vehicles drive

up. There were footsteps in the corridor and later th
vehicles trundled away. I left mama and walked past th
now-open door to papa's room. Yvonne was in ther
stripping the bed.

"I shall never forget your kindness," I said. "I sha
never be able to fully repay you."

She looked at me steadily for a moment and I realize
just how lovely this copper-skinned woman really wa.
Her face was flawless; her features added to a rare beauty
Her eyes were soft brown, not impelling but gentle an
understanding.

"*Mademoiselle,* I loved him too, in my own way."

I embraced her impulsively. "I know you did. Yo
made his life less lonely and it took courage to live her
after what has been happening over the years. Mama an
I didn't have that kind of courage."

"Perhaps your mama did not, but when you left her
you were too young to understand. Now you are grow
and you are going to remain. That takes courage."

"We must find out what is happening. We must get th
plantation back in business, even if the days are sad one
now. I intend to see that the hands do a full day
work. . . ."

Yvonne shook her head. "None will come here to wor
now. I know. They will be too afraid."

The thought had never occurred to me, but it was ver
likely true. "Then we'll have to do the best we can. If w
lose this year's crop, by next seeding time perhaps th
village men will change their minds or be driven to work
ing here because of a lack of money to live on. In an
event, the crop will somehow be harvested. Too late, o
course, but we shall never give up the plantation."

"Your papa, he would have liked to hear you say that
mademoiselle."

I sighed, because papa would never know. "We have t
plan the funeral. Mama is not capable of that so I wil
have to take over for her."

"Plan for a big funeral," she said, "for no man wa
better loved in the village."

"Yes, I rather agree with you. All the years we wasted, not being with him."

"It was his wish that you and your mama not be faced with the danger of this curse."

I said, "Suppose the curse is the cause of these deaths, Yvonne. How many more will die before it is satisfied?"

"There were fifty or more watching the wreck burn and the passengers and crew jump into the water. I do not know how many more. Only the ghost of that captain could answer you."

"You still believe his dying curse is the cause of this?" I asked.

"*Oui, mademoiselle.* I believe that. Perhaps I am wrong. It is possible because I grew up on an island where superstition is held in high regard and ghosts are as common as people."

"You speak well," I complimented her. "You must have had a fine education."

"It was good. My father was not poor until just before he died, when he lost everything. They say an enemy killed him by means of an *ouanga*. While he lived I went to school at a convent. After his death I had to find work. That is the story of my life, except to add that since coming to this plantation I have enjoyed the best moments of that life. The happiest and most satisfying."

"I'm pleased and I hope these moments will continue, Yvonne. Now I'd best go to mama and comfort her if I can."

"She will have need of you." Yvonne finished stripping the bed and she removed the medicine from the table beside the bed, placing the bottle in the pocket of her apron before going on to her next task in cleaning up the room.

Mama did find the courage to face things. By funeral time next day, she was dry eyed and steeled against the ordeal. Jeff came to do all he could, which was considerable. He'd already made the arrangements in a most satisfactory manner. Mama, Yvonne and I rode a hired hack to the village and the church. It came as somewhat of a shock to me, but the church was not half filled and there seemed to be few people on the streets. Of course, I didn't comment about this.

The services were simple and we followed the same hearse which had carried Jeff's father to the cemetery. There we stood beside the open grave while the final rites were spoken. When we turned away I was in time to see Hattie, again in her white dress, hat and shoes, simpering with self-satisfaction over another funeral.

Without a word I left mama and Yvonne and ran over to her side before she was able to get away. I seized her arm and confronted her in what I must admit was a blaze of anger.

"Why do you attend all funerals of victims of this curse? Why do you wear white when black is the color for sorrow? Who are you, anyway? Why did you threaten my life with a gun? Answer me, because you cannot remain silent about this the rest of your life. I will not permit you to do so."

Jeff and Dr. Shea were hurrying toward us. Jeff took my arm and Dr. Shea seized Hattie's right arm and turned her away. He glanced at me with a sharp shake of his head before he led the woman off.

I turned to Jeff and pressed my face against his shoulder. "I'm a fool," I said. "I shouldn't have done that. The poor woman can't be responsible for the way she acts."

"It's all right," Jeff said.

"I wasn't thinking. I was too filled with anger."

"At a time like this, nobody thinks well. And that woman is a weird one. She did threaten your life. You are not wholly to blame."

I saw mama and Yvonne getting into the hack for the ride home. Apparently they thought I was going to remain with Jeff.

"Will you take me home?" I asked.

"Of course I will." He led me away from the grave. His buggy was waiting a short distance down the slope. He helped me into it. I looked about for Dr. Shea but he'd apparently taken that poor, addled woman home.

"There were so few here," I said. "It was my impression that papa was well liked."

"Half the village moved away. They said they'd listened
that packet whistle once too often. Most of the people
re are scared. Others are getting ready to move. There
on't be much left I'm afraid."

"Then Yvonne was right. None of the men who agreed
come to work for me will ever show up."

"Nobody will. It's too bad. If that captain wanted the
wn destroyed, he's got his wish. I'm lucky. My office is
New Orleans. Even Dr. Shea will have to find some-
here else to practice because there won't be enough
ople left to support a doctor."

Jeff was allowing the horse to proceed at his own speed
ad, as a result, we rode slowly through the village and I
as able to see what it would soon look like. At the
ouses people had moved from only hours ago, doors were
ft open, and there were deep tracks of wagon wheels
cross the lawns as the heavy vehicles had been moved up
or loading. In some instances the white fences had been
orn up to make room for the wagons. At the homes of
eople who stayed, curtains were pulled, windows shut
nd they seemed almost as forlorn as the empty houses.

"It makes you realize a curse can really wreck a town
nd so many lives," Jeff said.

"I'm not going to be frightened away," I said firmly.
I'll manage somehow. Yvonne is going to stay with me
fter mama leaves."

"She'll be going today?"

"Almost at once. She didn't even want to return to the
lantation after the funeral, but common sense told her
he must, to arrange her things and to have a final talk
vith me."

"I'm glad Yvonne is staying with you."

"I'd be terrified if I had to stay in that house alone."

"You wouldn't have been alone, Carolyn."

"But I. . . ." I glanced at him. "Thank you, Jeff. You
re a dear. You planned to be close by, didn't you?"

"I planned better than that, if you would have agreed. I
vas going to ask you to marry me. Now, at once."

I leaned over and kissed his cheek. "I couldn't. Not
ow, Jeff."

"It wasn't just the idea of protecting you. I'm in lov
with you. I haven't the slightest doubt about that."

"Nor have I," I said softly. "No doubt of your lov
for me. Nor mine for you. But we cannot discuss this now
Kiss me just once, darling, and then take me back."

He brought the buggy to a halt along the lonely roa
to the plantation. He took me in his arms and for a lon
moment our lips met in a warm, enduring kiss, the swee
ness of which would remain with me the rest of my lif
Then, in deference to my sorrow—and his, for he'd burie
his father too only two days ago—he released me an
took up the reins. We didn't speak during the rest of th
ride.

TEN

As Jeff pulled up before the mansion, a tall, emaciate
man in a Prince Albert frock coat, high celluloid collar
black gloves, and, of all things, an old-fashioned stove pip
hat, arose from his seated position on the front steps. H
removed the hat and bowed low, swinging his arm in
graceful gesture that used to be fashionable, but had no
been in vogue for the past thirty years.

"William Spencer, Esquire, at your service, miss. Goo
afternoon to you, Mr. Horton. I trust you are both wel
and I grieve with you, Miss Carolyn, over the loss of you
father. He was a man I greatly admired."

Jeff said, "This is Willie Spencer, Carolyn. He is one o
two men who got off the packet the night it burned."

I found my hand taken very lightly in his black-glove
one and he bowed again. "I remember you as a little girl,

Miss Carolyn. You have become a most lovely young lady."

"Thank you," I said. "Won't you please come in?"

He smiled. A warm, friendly smile. "Your mother and our housekeeper suggested it might be best if I remained outside. I think they're afraid of me. I suppose I am unique. I haven't bought any new clothes in years, I'm afraid. And I have lived in solitude so long that I imagine not only look a bit queer but I probably am."

"You are anything but that, Mr. Spencer," I said. "I welcome you to my home and I wish you to come inside. Yvonne can, perhaps, offer you some food and certainly we can spare you a drink of brandy and . . . there are my father's cigars. He had quite a few of them and they have become quite useless to me. Would I presume too much if I asked you to accept them?"

"You may presume that I'll take them and welcome. Cigars, too, are a luxury I have long ago given up."

Yvonne made coffee and brought out a tray of delicious little frosted cakes. Her attitude was one of hostility until she watched Willie Spencer eating them and drinking coffee with the manners of high society. She was so impressed that when he left she presented him with a bag of the cakes. Yvonne, in her own way, was an extremely snobbish person, but she recognized a gentleman when she saw one, no matter what his dress.

"No," Willie Spencer said, in answer to my question, "I do not believe in curses. That night our captain—let me see now . . . his name was Palmer Haley, was it not, Mr. Horton?"

"Your memory is good," Jeff said.

"Well, Captain Haley was beside himself with terror. Yes, I said terror. He was worried to distraction when the river rose as the storm grew worse that night. Then the crevasse opened and the river poured through it taking the packet along as if it was a mere toy. When it grounded, the flood waters were all around us, rising, deep, dangerous. So many of us jumped overboard rather than be burned to death. I escaped and so did poor Ed Baker. We were both exceptionally strong swimmers and we were

heaven blessed, otherwise we'd never have made it. Cap
tain Haley was out of his mind when he screamed thos
curses. He was a madman if I ever saw one. But then, h
had reason to be. His wife and son were aboard and wei
bound to perish as did everyone else, save Ed Baker an
me."

"I'm grateful for learning some of the details," I said
"I never knew them before, Mr. Spencer."

"I lost my wife in the fire," he went on. "Ed Bake
lost his wife and two children. I know the tragedy turne
him into a man who drinks far too much. I believe he i
trying to forget. That is what I have been trying to do al
these years since it happened. You see, if I'd been witl
my wife that night, as I should have been, she might hav
escaped too. I blame myself for her death, because at th
time I was drinking and gambling and I left her alone ii
our cabin. I was never able to reach it."

"And do you agree, Mr. Spencer, that neither m
father nor any of the other people gathered to watch th
packet burn were able to reach the ship or rescue anyone?"

"Any who entered that swirling water, to swim or try
to row a boat, would have perished. There wasn't a chance
When I jumped clear of the ship I thought I was going to
die. I even wanted to die, but instinct is stronger than sor
row or the feeling of guilt. I swam and I was saved. Bu
this is the first time since then I have been able to face my
fellow man on anything but a basis for such routine trans
actions as buying food. I had money with me, in gold, anc
I am self-sufficient, so I had no problems. Except that I
was afraid to face anyone."

"If we'd known all that," Jeff said, "you'd have beer
more welcome in the village than you were, Mr. Spencer
I, at least, would have sought your friendship."

"Ah, that's a wonderful word. I came by because I fel
I had to express my condolences. Your father was a fine
man, Miss Carolyn."

He took his leave as politely as he had accepted oui
welcome and he walked away, a strange figure in his frock
coat and stovepipe hat, carrying two boxes of cigars and
the sack of cakes. We watched him until he disappeared.

"Do you think he meant what he said?" Jeff asked.

"Yes," I said in surprise. "Don't you?"

"I'm not sure. It would take a peculiar kind of man to live in seclusion for all those years and then come here with his story and his grand manners. We've regarded him as being as addled as Hattie. I find it hard to change my mind about him, yet he does act like a gentleman."

"He is a gentleman," I said.

Jeff nodded. "I think you're right. I'm going to call on him. He may be able to throw a little more light on the tragedy and maybe hazard a guess as to who might be carrying out the curse of Captain Haley. I intend to talk to him later today. We can't waste time now."

Cal Lindsay drove a carriage from the stables and left it in front of the mansion. He came in to greet us and inform us he was driving mama to the pier where a packet was due in about two hours. Yvonne called him to the second floor where she already had luggage packed and waiting.

Jeff said, "I'll be going back for a while. Expect me about six. We can talk then. You'll want to see your mother off now."

Mama came down presently and seated herself. In her traveling dress she was a lovely woman, now composed and as sure of herself as when we lived in New Orleans.

"I dread the thought of you being here alone," she told me. "I know there is little use in begging you to come with me, so I won't waste my time. Please be very careful, darling. Write often so I'll know you're safe. I have asked Yvonne to watch out for you and I'm sure she will do so. And I have invited her to come live with us in New Orleans if you decide to close this awful house. I never want to see it again."

"It's a beautiful house," I told her. "I love it. You will too, when time erases the many unpleasant memories you now have. I'll be careful. Jeff and Dr. Shea will be on hand if I need them. So will Cal Lindsay. We're all going to try and make this into a profitable plantation again."

"You never will," mama said. "I feel it in my bones

that nothing will ever come of this place—and rightly so, after what has happened."

Cal Lindsay came in to tell us it was time to go. I rode with mama to the pier and stayed with her until the packet pulled in, answering the signal Mr. Lindsay had set. While he carried luggage to the foot of the gangplank where the roustabouts took possession of it, I again assured mama I would be fine. I kissed her and stood on the pier to wave as the packet pulled away to the clanging of her bell and the booming sound of her whistle.

I thought then that this was not quite like the sound of the whistle which announced another victory for the captain's curse upon the village and those who had not gone to his aid. I forgot about that when my ankle began to pain me so that I cried out. I'd discarded the cane long ago, at Dr. Shea's suggestion, and while I limped a bit, I'd thought the ankle to be mending nicely. It was apparent that I'd been too active and now it was swelling and getting more and more painful. I hobbled to the carriage. Cal Lindsay caught up with me before I reached it and he helped me onto the seat.

"My ankle is still weak," I said. "I must have been on it too long. I'll be all right if I can get it up onto a chair for a while."

"Best you do that," he said. "Yvonne asked me to fetch provisions from the store. You feel up to waiting while I buy the things? I can bring you home first easy as not."

"No, Mr. Lindsay, I'll be fine. You go about getting whatever Yvonne needs. It will do me good to rest awhile."

"Got me another idea, miss. I'll let you off at Dr. Shea's office and you can see him about your ankle while I go to the general store."

"That's a fine idea. Dr. Shea will no doubt put another bandage on my ankle and I'll be grateful for it."

But Dr. Shea was not in his office, which, Cal Lindsay told me, was crowded with patients. The good doctor was on some emergency call and had left word to that effect. So I waited outside the general store until Mr. Lindsay had loaded the back of the carriage with supplies. Then he drove back at a leisurely pace. It was now late afternoon.

I was able to hobble inside. I called Yvonne but she didn't answer. Very likely she was out at the root cellar built well behind the house. She often spent time there selecting what she needed for the next meal.

Mr. Lindsay left everything in the kitchen and went off to attend to his own duties. I went upstairs to change my clothes and, for the first time, I felt the utter loneliness of this oversize mansion. It was not a place to be alone. I finished changing in time to welcome Jeff as he rode up in a buggy.

"You're limping again," he said.

"My ankle got tired, I guess. Mama is safely off and I was quite proud of the way she had composed herself. I am glad to see you, Jeff. I had a dreadful feeling of loneliness a little while ago. Of course, Yvonne is here so I shouldn't pay any attention to that sort of feeling, but it was there and I didn't like it."

"I've been out at the packet," he said, when we were seated in the drawing room. "Anse Austin's condition is worse and I have no doubt he'll soon die. That's when the whistle will blow again."

"I dread the sound of it, Jeff."

"I know. So do I, but this time we're going to find out if anybody does board the packet and somehow make the bell ring and the whistle blow. Of course, I don't mean that rusted whistle, but my thought is someone brings some kind of a whistle aboard and makes it work."

"I've thought of that too," I said.

"Well, if anybody sets foot on that packet in the next few days, I'll know it. I got me some pails of fine dust. It's been so long since it rained hereabouts that dust is the most plentiful thing in the parish. I sprinkled the dust all around the packet. On the decks, the gangplank, in the cabins. Unless we get a brisk wind to blow the stuff away, it will catch the footprints of anybody who comes aboard."

"Why, Jeff, that's a marvelous scheme. If we find footprints then we know a ghostly presence is not responsible for what has happened."

"That's what I want to prove. So now we wait . . . unfortunately, until Anse dies."

"Jeff," I said in sudden horror, "that means another person will grow ill. Someone always does. Anse became ill just before papa died. Now someone else will repeat that as Anse dies. It's horrible to think of it, but one must."

"Perhaps this time we'll be able to do something about it before there's yet another victim."

"I've been thinking about the whistle and the bell, Jeff. Have they ever sounded in the daytime?"

"No, never that I can recall." ·

"Then whatever creates that sound needs the protection of darkness. Does that seem like the work of a ghost?"

"I never thought it was, but I'll admit I never thought about the fact that the sounds always come by night. When someone dies by day, the whistle howls the night before, or the night after. I'm beginning to think my little trap is going to produce some results."

"I hope so. What time is it, Jeff?"

He snapped open the case of his watch. "Nearly six. It's been quite a day. A ghastly day, if you ask me."

"Yes, I agree. Poor papa! I wonder where Yvonne is? Have you heard her stirring about the kitchen?"

"No. In fact I forgot she was supposed to be here. I'll go look. You favor the ankle by staying on that sofa."

He came back in a few minutes, but not before I heard him run up the stairs to the second floor where he called Yvonne's name several times. He was frowning when he rejoined me.

"She's nowhere in the house that I can find."

"Maybe she changed her mind and decided not to stay here after all."

"No, that wouldn't be like Yvonne. She believes in ghosts and curses but, unlike us, she's used to them and she's not afraid of them. I wonder if she drove into the village for some reason."

"Let's ask Mr. Lindsay. I'll go along. My ankle is not too bad now." I stood up and tested it. The swelling had gone down and the pain considerably lessened. "It will do fine. Come on, I'm getting worried."

Cal Lindsay was at the stable and told us he hadn't seen Yvonne at all and that neither horse nor vehicle was missing. Returning to the house, Jeff and I searched the rooms for her and I paid special attention to her own room.

"I don't think any of her clothes are missing," I said. "Something's happened to her. Do you suppose she went to the packet?"

"I don't know," Jeff said. "It's been dark for an hour now. If she was anywhere outside she should have been back before now. I'd better have a look around. Are there lanterns?"

I led the way to the kitchen, where lanterns were kept on a shelf in a pantry cupboard. I insisted on going along, so we lit two of the lanterns and left by the kitchen door. We went first to the root cellar and found it closed. She was not inside and my worries began to grow rapidly. Yvonne was a person who followed a set pattern and vanishing like this, even for a few hours, was not like her.

"She may have grown suddenly ill. Perhaps a heart attack," I said.

"We'll find her close by, if that's the case. If she left the house for a brief period of time, where would she be apt to go? The root cellar, I suppose, but we've been there."

"She buries trash and garbage down the left path some distance from the house. She might have gone there."

We hurried along the path. Before we reached the spot where she buried the trash, we found her lying across the path. She was on her back, her eyes reflecting the dull glow of our lanterns, and she was dead. I sat down on the dry grass and broke into tears. I'd been through too much for one day and I was unable to control my sobbing.

Jeff lifted me to my feet. "We'll have to send Cal Lindsay for Dr. Shea. There's nothing we can do."

"What killed her?" I asked. "It was so sudden."

"From what I could see there's not a mark on her. As you say, perhaps a heart attack. Something very sudden. Dr. Shea will find out. There's nothing we can do for her now. Come along. I'll stay with you. There's nothing to fear. Her death has to be no more than a coincidence."

"Has she been dead long?"

"I don't know. I can't tell. I hope Cal didn't go off to the village."

We found him in his loft rooms above the stable. Aghast as he was at the news, he quickly saddled a horse and started for the village with the promise to hurry. Jeff and I walked slowly toward the house and we had almost reached it when that awful whistle sounded along with the clanging of the bell.

"It must be Anse," Jeff said.

"Jeff!" I cried out in horror. "Maybe it's for Yvonne!"

"Can you stand up to the walk out to the packet?"

"Yes. Yes, anything! We have to find out."

I supposed Cal Lindsay heard the whistle, but he would keep going to bring Dr. Shea back. Jeff and I walked as rapidly as my weak ankle would permit. It took us half an hour to reach the vicinity of the packet, but this time we carried lanterns and were able to light our way.

As I started ahead of Jeff to the gangplank, he grasped my arm and brought me to a halt. "The dust, remember? Let's look before we go aboard."

With our lanterns tilted to send the most light onto the rickety old gangplank, we moved along it inch by inch. Jeff had dusted it well. Not so deeply that the dust was too evident, but enough was there so that if anyone had set foot on this gangplank there'd have been clear signs of it. The dust was undisturbed.

We reached the deck and followed a trail of dust along it to the main salon, then to the hurricane deck and the pilothouse. The entire way had been dusted and, as at the gangplank, nothing had disturbed that layer of dust.

"That bell," Jeff pointed to the brass bell atop the pilothouse, "didn't ring. We know the whistle couldn't blow, but neither did any other whistle aboard this packet. Nobody set foot on it since I sprinkled the dust."

"What does that mean?" I asked him in growing horror.

"Either a bell and a whistle are sounded off the packet or . . . we are contending with some unearthly presence that can make those sounds without the use of the instruments that produce them. I do not favor the second theory. Let's look about on the knoll."

We found nothing there. Below the knoll, on the far side, was the rutted, narrow road leading to the main village road. We could see it in the weak moonlight.

"I don't know what to think," Jeff said. "We'd better get back to the house. Dr. Shea is likely there by now. Maybe he'll have some sort of a suggestion."

We started back, dismayed, puzzled and sorely worried. We were too weary and too concerned to speak, but Jeff held my hand in a tight grip and from it I drew what solace and courage I could muster.

Dr. Shea's buggy was in front of the house when we arrived, but neither he nor Mr. Lindsay was about. We heard them, finally, as they walked toward the rear of the mansion from the direction in which poor Yvonne's body lay. Jeff opened the kitchen door for them.

When they reached the kitchen, Mr. Lindsay said he was going back to the village for help. Dr. Shea closed the door and followed us into the drawing room.

"What happened to her?" I asked. As if I didn't know, after the sounding of the whistle and bell!

"I don't know," Dr. Shea said. He sat down like a weary, distraught man almost at the end of his endurance. "There isn't a mark on her. I would say it was her heart, except for two reasons."

"What are they?" Jeff asked.

"The fact that I was her doctor and I had occasion to examine her heart not long ago. It was strong and healthy. The second reason? The whistle and the damned bell. They seem to have diagnosed her death for me. Perhaps it's the same illness that struck down so many victims of the curse, and this time was simply more sudden. I have no way of knowing now, but the whistle and bell have not failed yet to tell me someone died in similar fashion to many other deaths here. I'm at my wit's end. And this death, unexpected as it was, will clear everyone out of the village who has so far resisted the urge to move in the last day or two. This village will soon cease to exist."

I said, "Doctor, perhaps Yvonne did die of natural causes. Is it the first death of this kind that happened so suddenly?"

"No, there were two others," Jeff broke in. "But they were clearly accidental deaths and easily accounted for, even if the whistle did blow."

"I'm wondering if the whistle could have meant the death of Anse Austin," I said.

Dr. Shea jumped to his feet. "I never gave it a thought. I'll drive over there at once and make certain. You two stay here. Watch over her, Jeff. Don't take any chances with anyone."

"I don't intend to," Jeff assured him and me. "We'll be here when you get back."

"Doctor, what makes you so apprehensive about me?" I asked.

"I saw Ed Baker staggering toward the village on my way out here. He was very drunk and it looked to me as if he'd been out in the vicinity of the wreck. At least that's the direction from which he appeared to have come."

"We'll look into that later," Jeff said. "Thanks for warning us."

Dr. Shea hurried out to his buggy while Jeff locked the door and then went to the kitchen to bolt that door as well. We returned to the drawing room and sat down. People would be here from the village soon to take care of Yvonne's body. Dr. Shea would return with news from Anse Austin. I found myself worried about an awful thing. That Dr. Shea would find Anse alive, meaning the packet whistle had not been meant for him. To have its strange influence reach this mansion again so soon was almost impossible to bear. I leaned weakly against Jeff and placed my head on his shoulder. His arm was around me and I felt safe, but my worries kept growing.

It took some time before my nerves were brought under control and my trembling and spells of sobbing openly were mastered. Jeff never left my side and, despite all my sorrow and my terror, I realized that I had been in love with him from the first and I was now more sure of it than ever.

"I've been thinking about something," he said. Mostly he talked to take my mind off what had happened. "Several townspeople who were at the scene of the burning packet all those years ago moved out of town during the time this so-called curse was in effect and others were dying. Yet, none of those who moved away died. At least not that I know of, but their deaths would surely have been reported here."

"Then this curse doesn't seem to reach beyond the village and the plantations," I said, quickly following his line of thought. "Jeff, a true ghostly curse would reach anywhere if the fantastic tales about them are true. More and more I'm convinced there is a human element behind all these deaths."

"Possibly," he admitted. "Certainly the fact that those who left town survived has some meaning, however vague at the moment. I'm disappointed that there were no footprints in the layers of dust I spread over the wreck."

"So am I. If there had been any, then we'd have been positive that a human vengeance seeker is responsible and not some phantom come back from the dead."

"True. I'd also like to know how a steam whistle is sounded where there is no boiler and no steam. The bell could be explained. Anybody could cart a bell around and ring it, but not a steam boiler, and from what I know of a whistle as large and loud as the one we hear, it can't be sounded without the use of steam."

"And that fact makes it seem the act of a ghost," I said.

We heard approaching vehicles and we went out to greet the people from the village with the now-all-too-familiar hearse. They decided to wait until Dr. Shea returned from Anse Austin's plantation so he could supervise the removal of Yvonne's body. Jeff and I returned to the house, leaving Cal Lindsay to stay with the authorities.

Dr. Shea returned shortly afterward and soon the grim procession passed the mansion. Dr. Shea turned back to give us the news about Anse.

"He's getting weaker and I've given up hope for him, but he's alive and that whistle wasn't meant to announce his death, that's sure."

"Then it *was* meant for Yvonne," I said. "I don't see why she would fall under that old curse. No one could blame her for not helping, for I doubt she was capable of it."

"Which reminds me," Jeff said with a frown. "She is the first woman to die. The first woman whose death was greeted by the ship's whistle."

"You're right," Dr. Shea said. "Please excuse me. I've got to be on hand when they bring Yvonne in. I want to examine her most carefully."

"All the others," I said, "died after lingering illnesses, most of which lasted for months. Except for two victims of accidents. Yvonne died very suddenly. Please let us know what you find, Doctor. And will you arrange for Yvonne to be buried in the family plot? Papa would have seen to that and I'm sure mama will agree it's proper."

"Of course," Dr. Shea said. "I'll see to it at once. Expect me back in the morning. Maybe this time we will find something to help solve this riddle."

He drove away quickly so he might overtake the procession. Jeff and I returned to the drawing room. It seemed to me we'd not eaten in hours, so I made coffee and found some of Yvonne's biscuits to heat.

Jeff looked so weary he appeared ill. I hadn't noticed that until now, when we faced one another across the kitchen table.

"You must get some rest," I told him. "I want you to go home, darling. I'll be all right here."

"I don't want to leave you, Carolyn."

"There is nothing in this house to harm me, Besides, Mr. Lindsay will be close by."

"I do have some letters that must go out tomorrow morning," he admitted.

"You've been giving me so much of your time your business will suffer. Please . . . don't worry about me."

"So long as Cal is here. . . ."

He was admitting his exhaustion in a roundabout way. Even if he remained, there'd be no rest for him because he'd be too uneasy and too intent on looking out for me. This was a time when I felt I must be self-reliant and I insisted again that he go.

I stood in the doorway watching the night swallow him up. Then I closed the door and walked slowly into the drawing room.

I'd never felt so alone in my life.

ELEVEN

The drawing room seemed to have increased in size, and its dark corners, beyond the range of lamp or candle-light, held the unnerving prospect of being hiding places for ghosts, or whatever malevolent creatures were the cause of all this terror.

I sat down, wondering how I'd find the courage to go upstairs and try to sleep. I couldn't imagine letting myself drift off in this atmosphere of death. As I sat there, little sounds, which no doubt had always existed in the still of night, now seemed strange and ominous to me. I had to do something. I began walking toward the front door and before I reached it I was all but running. I threw it open hoping to see Cal Lindsay somewhere close by. All I saw was intense darkness.

I closed the door again and bolted it. This didn't make me feel any safer. I went to the kitchen and did the dishes left after my light meal with Jeff. I tried to think of him and my love for him, but even that didn't overpower the fear of the darkness and the terror of being alone in this house. I was close to panic and I knew it.

If Yvonne had fallen under the vengeance of the dead packet captain, she was the first woman to die for that reason, as Jeff had stated and Dr. Shea agreed. Perhaps the pattern was changing. Perhaps I would be next, though

I'd not been among those who refused to go out to the packet. I had been no more than a little girl, but then Yvonne certainly hadn't been capable of helping either.

All this uneasiness compelled me to do something drastic, something which would probably terrify me even more, but I needed to prove to myself that I could fight this fear. I went upstairs, carrying a lamp. I lit two lamps in the corridor. I deliberately opened the door to the room where papa had died. Yvonne had straightened it up so that it looked all ready for papa when he returned from the fields or the sugar house. I closed the door as softly as if he were asleep in the bed.

I walked briskly toward Yvonne's room at the end of the corridor. Here the door was open. I went inside and lit two lamps before I looked around. Yvonne had been extremely neat and nothing was out of place. Certainly she could not have had any premonition of her death. I pulled open a closet door. There were two of them, I knew. One was of medium size, and the second, which I was now going to examine, was a walk-in of quite large proportions. I didn't walk in. I stared in some awe and mostly renewed fear at what I now saw for the first time.

Yvonne had converted this closet into a sort of miniature chapel. It contained an altar—a plain table with a white cloth over it—and on this were objects probably relating to whatever religion she was secretly in the habit of practicing.

There was a shallow white bowl and a somewhat battered goblet of what seemed to be pewter. Between these two objects lay a dagger with a pearl handle and a rather long, slim blade. Directly behind this and in the center of the altar was a glass bowl containing fruit, two withered carrots, and a small bottle containing a dark liquid.

I brought the lamp closer to inspect some discolorations on the dagger. I shuddered because the stains looked to me like dried blood. I peered into the pewter goblet. At the bottom of it was a thickening of what I knew must be blood.

I backed out of the closet slowly and closed the door. I left the room and went to my own. I'd hoped to have gained some courage from my deliberate entry into her room and papa's, but I discovered I was more distraught than ever.

I prepared for bed, nervously poised to flee at the first sign of any intruder, human or ghostly. I wondered if I'd have the nerve to blow out the lamps. I went to a window overlooking the front of the mansion. There was moonlight. Not much, but enough to show me a man slowly pacing across the front of the mansion. He carried a gun held in the crook of his arm. It was Cal Lindsay and some of my terror abated. I should have known he'd be watching over me, and when his spell of duty ended, Jeff would be there. Perhaps even Dr. Shea would take his turn. I made up my mind that I was foolish to give way to fear. I slipped into bed, blew out the last lamp and lay back to seek sleep.

It didn't come swiftly or easily, but finally I dozed and then I must have fallen into a deep sleep for I didn't open my eyes again until the room was filled with morning sunlight.

I hurried to look out, in case there were carriages or buggies indicating I had visitors, but there was none. Cal Lindsay was no longer patrolling, but I knew he wouldn't be far away.

I washed and dressed, taking no time to arrange my hair elaborately. I pulled it tight and tied it with a ribbon before I went downstairs and made my breakfast. I still felt a sense of loneliness, but by day it was not as severe and it didn't bring on imagined sounds or flitting shadows.

I entered papa's library, which also served as his office. I sat behind his desk and began going through it. I had to make some sense out of all of his papers and books so that, if I could find workers, I could get the plantation in order. There was such a thing as importing men to work the fields and, not having been as close to the tragedies that had occurred over the years as the village men had, they might not be so adversely affected by the idea of a curse on the plantation and the town.

Within an hour I realized that while papa had suffered severe reverses due to crop failure and the lack of a product from his sugar house, he was still quite a wealthy man when he died. There'd be much to do in straightening out his estate. Perhaps mama could take care of some of it in New Orleans. Jeff and Dr. Shea would help me here, so I anticipated no undue trouble.

Jeff, looking refreshed, arrived late in the morning and he was met by Cal Lindsay. They talked for a few minutes and then both came toward the house. I let them in and greeted Jeff with a resounding kiss that made Mr. Lindsay grin.

"I've something to show you," I said, "but it will keep. Mr. Lindsay, you have my gratitude for watching over me last night. I saw you walking back and forth."

"It's little enough, Miss Carolyn," he said. "Jeff just brought some bad news from the village," he added, more somberly.

"Only a few people are left," Jeff said, "and they're going as soon as they can find wagons to carry their things. The stores have closed and in a few more days it will be a dead village."

"Which means," Mr. Lindsay added, "we won't be able to get anybody to come here and work the farm. If the crop isn't cut in the next week it'll be ruined. What might be best is to burn the crop and plow everything under. If we can find anybody to do the plowing."

"It is discouraging," I admitted, "but we can weather it, Mr. Lindsay. All I hope is that you won't leave too."

"Not likely," he said with a smile. "I spent most of my life here and I'm not leaving. I don't scare easy and I don't give any thought to the curse of a dead man. I'm here to stay as long as you'll have me, Miss Carolyn."

"Thank you. With both of you to help I'll get the plantation back into business next year. I'm discounting this year's crop entirely."

Jeff handed me an envelope. "This came this morning. It's from your mother, according to the return address. She must have written it right after the packet left and mailed it yesterday at the first stop down the river."

"Thank you," I said again. "It seems all I do is thank

you. Both of you. May I be excused for a few moments while I read the letter?"

"We've plenty to talk about," Jeff said. "Cal and I agree that you won't have to give up the plantation and we're going to figure out ways to make sure you don't."

Mama's letter wasn't long and she had written it as the packet left because she wanted me to get it today. Mailing it at the first stop would insure that. She hated herself for leaving me but her state of nerves was such that she found it impossible to remain. I was glad that she had not, for she would likely have been a care and I needed all the time I could find to devote to running down the truth behind all these strange deaths. And to familiarize myself with the operation of a large sugar plantation such as this.

Mama also revealed that papa had arranged, upon his death, that a considerable amount of cash be placed at her disposal until the estate was settled. So she was comfortably well off. She was reconciled to the fact that I wouldn't be back in New Orleans for some time because she had prepared two trunks of my clothes and would ship them off at once. Mama always had been a great help when she set her mind to it, and was not befuddled with fears and with sorrow.

When I returned to the drawing room from the library, I was in time to admit Dr. Shea who had just arrived. I sat down while Dr. Shea told us about the death of Yvonne.

"I did an autopsy," he said. "It was required by law because of the strangeness of the circumstances surrounding her death. I found no evidence of foul play, no marks, not even a scratch. I sent the contents of her stomach for analysis and I should get a report by tomorrow, for I used a special messenger who is to wait for the results and bring them back to me."

"Then her death is like all the others," Jeff said. "Unexplainable."

"No, not quite, for she is the first to die suddenly."

"Except for John Morgan, who was kicked by a horse and killed, and Larry Fletcher, who broke his neck falling off the roof of his barn," Cal Lindsay said.

"Yes, but those deaths were easily explained," Dr. Shea said. "Yvonne's was not. It's a real mystery to me."

"I wonder why she died out there on the path," Jeff said. "If there was no heart failure she couldn't just have dropped dead. Or could she, Doctor?"

"I don't know," Dr. Shea admitted. "Perhaps the report from Baton Rouge will give us some hint, though I learned nothing from other specimens I sent there. Meantime, Yvonne's funeral is set for this afternoon. I thought this haste was necessary because otherwise there might not be anyone to help with the funeral. I'm sure she had no relatives that we know of, so there was no need to wait."

"No need," I agreed. "I'll be ready."

"Have you heard how Anse Austin is this morning, Doctor?" Cal Lindsay asked.

"I just came from there. I don't think he'll last much longer. A week, maybe."

Cal Lindsay made a steeple of his hands as he plunged into deep thought. He was not a quick thinker, but his ideas were sometimes very useful. Papa always said that.

"Now," Cal said, "with nobody left in the village, where does the curse go from here? Nobody remains but us, and Anse's son."

"Perhaps this is what the dead captain had in mind," I said. "The destruction of the entire village."

"What about Ed Baker and Willie Spencer?" Jeff asked. "Did they leave too?"

"I don't know," Dr. Shea said. "Ed Baker was around last night, happily drinking himself into a stupor because this time he had an excuse for getting drunk. He kept talking about the end of the village, but it was not possible to tell whether he was sad over it or gloating. Willie never put in an appearance."

"I certainly wouldn't trust Ed Baker," I said, "but I'm not afraid of Mr. Spencer. I believe him to be a fine man, brought down by the tragedy that took his family."

"What of Hattie?" Cal Lindsay inquired. "Has she left too?"

"We'll surely find out this afternoon," Dr. Shea said with a grimace. "If she's around she'll be at the funeral."

"I wonder," Jeff said thoughtfully.

"What do you mean?" I asked.

"She only appears at the funerals of those we regard as victims of Captain Haley's raving curse. Perhaps the death of Yvonne isn't one of those."

"She must have been, Jeff," I said. "Don't you remember how the whistle sounded?"

"I still can't see how she was involved or fell under the curse," Jeff insisted.

"If I can reach Hattie—that is, if she appears—I'll do my best to find out what she knows," I vowed. "This time she won't get away from me."

"Nor me," Jeff said. "No matter how addled she is, that woman owes us an explanation. If she didn't know anything about the deaths, she wouldn't come to the funerals. If she attended every funeral, I'd think differently, but she does not."

Dr. Shea said, "With people of as unsound a mind as Hattie appears to have, there's no telling what they will do. Or why. Which reminds me, Carolyn. You were to tell us something. . . ."

"Oh, yes. In Yvonne's room. I'd like to know what it means. If you will all follow me. . . ."

I led them upstairs and opened the door of the large closet in Yvonne's room.

"Good heavens," Cal Lindsay cried out. "That's voodoo. It's a religion practiced in Haiti and Jamaica. I was there once, in my younger days when I went to sea. They make sacrifices before altars like this."

"Yvonne, practicing that sort of thing?" Dr. Shea asked in wonder.

"I'll tell you what I think," Jeff said. "She was using this to try to overcome the influence of Captain Haley's bitter revenge against almost everyone in the village."

"That could be," I agreed. "She did mention once, I think, about the mysteries of this religion, or whatever it is. She seemed to take considerable stock in it too."

Dr. Shea examined the contents of the pewter goblet and wrinkled his face in distaste. "This is blood all right. Well congealed, so it must have been drawn at least two or three days ago. I suggest you have all this gathered up and destroyed, Carolyn."

"Perhaps, but later. When everything is cleared up and we know why and how all these people died."

"As you wish. I might remind you that it's getting time for the services," Dr. Shea said.

"I'll dress at once, if you gentlemen will wait downstairs."

It didn't take me long. I wore the same black dress, gloves and hat which I'd used at papa's funeral. By the time I came downstairs, Cal Lindsay had the carriage waiting. As chief mourner, I would transfer to a hack in the village, he informed me. So I rode with Jeff and Dr. Shea followed us.

It was eerie riding along Main Street. Everything was boarded up. No stores were open and there wasn't a soul on the streets. A few abandoned dogs wandered about, unable to reconcile themselves to being without a family. No one was at the church and Jeff, Dr. Shea and Cal Lindsay, along with the hearse driver, had to act as pallbearers. The village clergyman, a man devoted to his calling, had not yet left out of deference to holding these rites.

The church service was brief. As we approached the cemetery I looked for Hattie, but there was only one person standing at the foot of the newly dug grave. In his frock coat and high beaver hat, Willie Spencer looked, for the first time, as if he belonged on the scene.

Hattie never did appear and I began to think that Jeff was right. That she was only interested in those who died by the wish of Captain Haley, himself dead so many years ago. Yet, the packet whistle had blown and its bell sounded a knell for Yvonne. It made no sense in relation to what had gone on at all the other funerals.

Afterward, it turned out that Willie Spencer had dug the grave and was there to fill it in. No other person from the village would consent to this chore. Papa's death was the inspiration for all to leave and Yvonne's untimely end only spurred them on.

"The poor woman was kind to me more than once," Willie advised us. "She used to give me hot food and little presents to take home. I didn't need them, but she wasn't aware of that and her kindness was genuine. Helping put her to rest was little to do in compensation."

"Have you seen anything of Hattie?" I asked.

"No. It's strange she didn't appear. She never missed one before."

"Perhaps we should pay her a visit," I suggested, "just to make certain she's all right."

We all agreed. While I waited in the hack, which Cal Lindsay drove because the regular driver was gone, the others completed filling in the grave. Willie Spencer accepted my invitation to ride with me and we and Jeff headed for Hattie's cabin with Dr. Shea driving behind us in his buggy.

"Have you seen Ed Baker?" Jeff asked Willie.

"Not in the last two or three days," Willie replied. "But then, he's been drinking even more lately so I suspect he's sleeping it off somewhere. Unless he joined the exodus."

"Would you consider Ed Baker capable of murder?" Jeff asked.

Willie thought about that for a few seconds. "I'd consider him capable of anything when he's drunk. I've seen him like a wildman on occasion. But if you are asking if Ed is guilty of these deaths, I would say no. They have been subtly done and Ed Baker is not capable of being subtle about anything. He might break a man's head or shoot him down, but he couldn't kill a man by a means that is so far undetectable."

"Do you have any ideas who might be guilty?" I asked him.

"None, Miss Carolyn. I only wish I did."

We came into sight of Hattie's cabin. Dr. Shea pulled alongside the hack and leaned over to talk to us.

"Let me go on ahead. She trusts me and knows me. Even if she doesn't let me in, I doubt I'd run any risk of being shot and I'll find out whether or not she's there."

"That's a good idea," I told him. "I know what you mean, Doctor, after having faced the wrong end of Hattie's gun. I'd be mighty timid about approaching the cabin myself."

He nodded and drove on. A hundred yards from the cabin, we saw him alight and heard him call out Hattie's name. A curtain was pulled to one side and the gun barrel was poked out to cover Dr. Shea. He came to an abrupt stop. He spoke to her, though we couldn't hear what he said. After a few moments he advanced to within a dozen feet of the house and then halted abruptly as if he'd been ordered to do so. There was more talk and then he turned around and went back to his buggy. Once again he pulled up beside the hack. This time he got out and stood looking up at us.

"She's all right. Bodily, that is. Mentally I think she's worse. She told me she did not attend the funeral of Yvonne because she never goes to the services for a woman. Only men, she said. And she told me to warn everyone that she does not intend to leave, even though I advised her the town was already abandoned."

"I never thought of that," I said. "How will she survive? There'll be no way for her to get food."

"I reminded her of that too, and she told me the Lord would provide."

"She'll die in there," I said. "We can't leave her alone."

"I think you might find that to be necessary," Dr. Shea said. "She also warned me that the next person who comes within range of her gun is going to be shot. She means it. She's a dangerous woman and I would under no circumstances try to force her out of that cabin, no matter for what purpose. It's true, she may die there. She's stubborn enough to do that very thing, but anyone who tries to save her from her own foolishness is liable to die too. Remember, she means every word."

"Then let her stay there," Cal Lindsay grumbled from his seat outside the coach. "I know I won't risk my life to help her."

"Well," I said, "we don't have to do anything for her at the moment. Mr. Lindsay, would you be kind enough to drive me home now. Jeff, your buggy is at the plantation, so you'll have to return with me. Doctor, you are invited to supper if you wish to come."

"I can't, thank you, Carolyn. I've got my hands full at the moment."

"Doing what, Doc?" Lindsay asked. "There's nobody left to be sick."

"I'm packing everything," Dr. Shea said, "I'm moving too. There's no point in my staying here."

"Oh, Doctor," I said, "I'm sorry to hear that. I hope you won't go too far away."

"Only to the next village, and I won't leave for a few more days anyway."

"I'll miss you," I said.

"I doubt it," he said with a smile. "I'll be around as often as you'll have me. And, I might add, I'll have to remain until Anse Austin's condition goes one way or the other. He is in no shape to be moved."

"I'd forgotten all about Anse," Jeff admitted.

"I'm going there now," Dr. Shea said. "I'll come by on my way to the village and tell you about his condition. But I won't remain for supper, if you will excuse me."

We drove off as he returned to his buggy. In the village we transferred to our carriage but we were delayed when Mr. Lindsay had to stable the horses that pulled the hack. We became acutely aware of that duty when we reached the village and found the hearse driver busily loading the vehicle with his furniture. He already had two coffins lashed to the top of the hearse.

"The hack and the horse belong to him," Jeff said. "He'll likely take the horse with him so we won't have to worry about seeing it's cared for."

Willie Spencer left us right after we cleared the outskirts of the village. He promised to come by from time to time and he intended to search for Ed Baker.

"Well," Jeff asked as we rode the rest of the way, "what's next?"

"Tomorrow," I said, "I intended to see what's to be done about the cane. Mr. Lindsay advises burning it and I'm beginning to think he's right."

"It's a good way to clear the fields, Carolyn, and you're not going to get any part of the crop in, that's sure. By next spring things ought to change."

"I hope so, because no matter what happens, I will not give up this plantation," I said. "I owe that much to papa for the way mama and I neglected him when he needed us most."

"He sent you away," Jeff reminded me.

"That doesn't matter. We should have guessed something was wrong and come back despite him. Perhaps he'd be alive today if we had. I failed him that time, but I won't fail the plantation he worked so hard to establish."

"In that case," Jeff said quite solemnly, "I think I'll enjoy being a sugar-cane farmer."

TWELVE

It had grown dark before Jeff and I finished supper and talked for a long time, trying to formulate some kind of plan for beginning anew with the plantation. We well realized, however, how hopeless any planning was in the face of this unsolved mystery. It had already caused so many strange deaths and had driven the population of an entire village away. Unless, and until, these people returned, running the plantation would be impossible. And, as if this type of planning was not difficult enough, our plans for marriage were even harder to contemplate.

"We'll have to wait," Jeff said grimly, "until it's all settled. Until people return to their homes and agree to work on the plantation. And, I might add, until that wreck from which all this trouble seems to come is forever destroyed."

"I mentioned that to papa before he died and he was strongly against it, darling."

"I know somebody was, because I'd advocated burning the thing long ago. Why did he oppose it?"

"He said if there were ghosts and if the old packet was their earthly home, he hadn't the heart to destroy it."

Jeff looked his surprise. "I thought he didn't believe in ghosts."

"He didn't," I said with a sigh. "But like so many people who do not believe in them, he still feared them. Or respected them. I'm not sure which."

"What about you? Do you believe in them?"

"No," I said. "Right now I do not. But don't ask me around midnight when I'm trying to get to sleep alone in this big old house. While I keep listening for the sound of the ship's bell and its whistle. About that time I half believe."

"Tonight," he said, "sleep well and don't be afraid. I'll be outside, well armed and wide awake. If you even think you hear anything, simply place a lighted lamp or candle in any window. I'll be at your side in less than a minute."

"Thank you, Jeff," I said. "It is comforting to know someone is close by I can depend upon."

He arose and offered to help me with the supper dishes, a gesture I quickly rejected because I wanted to do something to help make me tired enough that sleep might come easily. We were at the door when we heard Dr. Shea's buggy drive up. We went out into the cool night air to meet him.

"I'm not staying," he said. "I just came by to tell you Anse is worse. It's only a matter of a short time."

"Before we hear that awful whistle," I said.

"Yes. No doubt it will sound. Are you riding to town, Jeff?"

"No," Jeff said. "I'm going to stay here and patrol the premises. I think Carolyn needs some measure of protection."

"Count on me for tomorrow night," Dr. Shea said. "I take it, from the way you stand there holding hands like a couple of love-smitten children, that you two are in love."

"Yes," I said, "we are."

"I'm happy for both of you and full of sadness for myself. I'd hoped I might stand a chance, but of course that would have been impossible anyway. You have to run a sugar plantation and I have to be a doctor. I doubt the two would join easily. I'll not return to this village anyway. Not now. Not even if all the good people return. However, I will not leave until I know you're safe, Carolyn, and until we finally discover what has caused so many of my patients to die despite all I could do to save them. It's a mystery I cannot tolerate. Good night, then. It's going to be a lonely village."

He drove off. Jeff brought me back to the door. "The doctor was in love with you, wasn't he?"

"Yes, I'm sure he was."

"He still is, my dear. I have to feel sorry for him because I feel so much happiness for myself. Good night. I'll be right outside. Any lighted window will bring me in a hurry."

I drew my arms around his neck and kissed him with all the love at my command. It was a long and lingering kiss that said so much without words. Jeff stepped back, smiled warmly and let go of my hand. I entered the house and closed the door but I didn't bolt it. Jeff had told me Cal Lindsay had provided him with a key. If Jeff had to get inside quickly, there was nothing to slow him down.

I did the dishes, straightened the kitchen and I was about to blow out all but the lamp I would carry upstairs when I heard a scratching at the back door. For a moment my heart ceased to beat and that old fear began to creep through my system.

"Carolyn," a whispered voice said, "it's Randy. Let me in. It's important."

I peered out the window set in the top of the door and saw that it was Randy before I turned the key and let him in. He scuttled over to a chair beside the table and sat down.

"I know Jeff is out there and I don't want him to see me. He's got a gun, did you know that?"

"I suspected he might have, and you're very foolish to slip past him. If he'd seen you he might have fired."

"Jeff's a city man. He don't know anything about the

country. I can move all around him in the night and he'll never know I was there. I had to talk to you."

"Then please tell me why you came, Randy. I'm very tired. This has been an exhausting day for me."

"Burying that colored woman who worked for your pa? I didn't like her very much. I don't think she liked me, either."

"That's not what you came to tell me, Randy." I was beginning to be a bit afraid of him. His hair was awry, his face covered with perspiration showing how he'd moved very fast through the night and probably worried about being seen. There was a look of desperation in his eyes.

"No," he acknowledged, "you're right. I came to ask you to marry me."

I sat down abruptly at the table across from him. "Randy, I'm sorry, but I'm not in love with you."

"I know that. I'm in love with you though. Papa asked me to come and talk to you."

"Your father asked you to come?"

"Yes. He's going to die pretty soon and he knows it all right. He said it's always been his dream to join our two plantations and when he dies, ours will belong to me. If we marry we can merge them. We'll have the biggest plantation in the parish, maybe the whole state. You got to have help in running this place and you don't know anything about it. Even if you did, a girl can't take charge of a big place like this. . . ."

"Randy, I'm going to marry Jeff Horton and together we'll run this plantation. I have no plans to merge it with yours and I'm sorry if you and your father ever hoped I would."

His lean face darkened. "You may be mighty sorry you didn't throw in with me."

"I doubt it, Randy. Please go now. By the front door so Jeff can see you and not take a shot at you, which he might if you slip out the back."

"I wouldn't care if he shot me," Randy said in a mixture of anger and disappointment. "I'm leaving like I came and he won't see me."

"I'd rather you left openly."

"Well, I won't. Maybe he'll see me and think you asked me to come over secretly. Wouldn't that be somethin'?"

"Good night," I said. "You may leave by any means you wish. I only ask that you do not come back."

"Before this is over you'll be askin' my help. Wait and see. Besides, I'll be as important as you when papa dies. I'll own a plantation near as big as yours. And I'll make more money, and hire more hands, and I'll be looked up to."

I walked out of the kitchen, carrying the lamp. I did hesitate a moment and when I pushed the door open again, I was in time to see the back door close softly. I went to it and turned the key. Looking out of the window I saw no trace of Randy and, as there was no commotion or hail from Jeff, I guessed that Randy had slipped by him. I shivered at the thought of being harried by this foolish and egotistical young man and I hoped I'd sent him out of my life forever.

I went directly to my bedroom, lit more lamps, took down my hair and gave it about half the regulation number of brushings. I was very tired. Moments later I slipped into bed. I blew out the bedside lamp and settled down.

The house was quiet. I knew Jeff was outside, but I felt uneasy. I kept turning restlessly, trying to rid myself of this unaccountable fear. There were no sounds anywhere. I knew Jeff was right outside and yet the apprehension persisted.

I finally sat up to listen and I thought I heard a creak from the direction of the grand staircase. A few of the stairs did make faint sounds when they were subjected to weight. By day I wouldn't even have heard it but by night, when the silences are so complete, the sound did reach me.

I hastily lit the bedside lamp and put on a robe and slippers. Clutching the lamp, I left my bedroom and moved toward the stairs.

From the top of them I could look down at the shadowy form standing in the reception hall looking up at me.

I found my voice somehow. "What do you want? Who are you?"

The low laugh startled me as much as if there'd been a scream of rage directed at me.

"Randy?" I asked in a hoarse whisper.

"Come on downstairs," he said. "I ain't going to hurt you."

I slowly descended the steps, still not certain this was Randy.

"Didn't you leave the house?" I asked.

"I stepped into the pantry, that's all."

I was a dozen steps above him now. "I don't know what you wish of me, or why you did this foolish thing, but I am now asking you to leave this house at once."

"Oh, sure. I'm goin'. By the front door. I'm goin' to slip out like a burglar . . . or like a man sneakin' away from his ladylove. That's what I want Jeff to think. I ain't goin' to let you marry him. We got to merge these plantations like pa wants and I don't care what I have to do to get that done."

I slowly descended the rest of the stairs and walked on by him. I went to one of the front windows and pulled aside the drapery before I placed the lamp on a small table so its light shone through the window.

Almost at once I heard Jeff coming at a dead run, but Randy did not. He was too engrossed in trying to put over his idea that when Jeff saw him leave he'd think ill of me and abandon our plans for marriage. It was the silly scheming of an immature mind, but Randy truly seemed to believe it.

The key was thrust into the front-door lock and the door was flung open. Randy backed away from the threat of the rifle in Jeff's hands.

I said, "Randy paid me a secret visit about an hour and a half ago, asking me to marry him so that our plantations could be merged. I thought he'd left, but he merely hid and waited until now."

"Are you crazy?" Jeff said harshly to Randy. "I might have killed you."

"He fancies himself so good a woodsman that you'd never have seen or heard him until he wished you to. He came back in order to leave in the dead of night and be seen by you as he slipped out of the house. It was his idea that you would then believe that I had asked him here and that you would no longer wish to marry me."

Jeff carefully placed the rifle across one of the reception hall chairs. Then he seized Randy by the nape of his neck and the seat of his pants and propelled him violently to and out the front door, hurling him onto the lawn so that he fell, sprawling across the grass.

Jeff said, "If you come back here, or you speak to Miss Carolyn again, I'll break your jaw, Randy. That's a promise. Now get out of here and thank your luck you're leaving in one piece. Get out!"

Randy got up somewhat painfully and for a moment I thought he might go completely insane and try to attack Jeff. He must have mastered the urge with little effort for he turned around and walked away, shoulders sagging, his steps slow, until Jeff yelled at him. Randy broke into a lumbering run and vanished into the night. I sat down weakly.

"That boy must be mad," I said. "Perhaps bearing up under his father's hopeless condition did that to him."

"Don't be that charitable," Jeff said. "He's only interested in the merging of the two plantations, which would make him a great big man once his father died and he controlled both farms. I doubt he's dangerous, but then you never can tell and I'd be very wary of him from now on."

"If I never see him again I'll be quite satisfied, thank you. Jeff, aren't you going to say anything else?"

"What?" he asked. "What should I say?"

"Aren't you going to ask me if I really didn't send for him so that I might make you jealous?"

He burst out laughing. "Now, if that had been Dr. Shea, things might have had a different aspect. But Randy? I know you love me and it won't matter one whit to me if Randy, or even Dr. Shea, calls in the middle of the night, with you looking so fetching with your hair down and in a nightgown."

"It wouldn't matter?" I asked indignantly.

"Not after I broke his neck."

I hugged him and kissed him and decided I wasn't sleepy after all. We lit more lamps and found that now we could talk and make plans. In the face of what seemed to be impending disaster for the plantation we decided that Jeff would turn his New Orleans office over to subordinates and trust them to handle his affairs while he devoted his time to helping me get the plantation on a profitable basis. If villagers did not return when this terror was over, then we'd buy that part of the village we required and we would import other workers and their families.

We also decided that under no circumstances would we ever join this plantation with that of Randy Austin.

Jeff left, taking his rifle and assuring me he'd be more careful, for he blamed his lack of vigilance on Randy gaining access to the house. I went to bed, oblivious to anything other than the plans Jeff and I had made, and I slept soundly.

In the morning the episode with Randy Austin seemed more pathetic than ominous, but I still felt angry over his wild assertions and scheming. It occurred to me that from the moment that Randy's father died—and it would be soon—Randy would be in danger of losing the plantation left to him, rather than adding to it. He was adult enough to take over the operation but I doubted he had the mental capacity to do so. Especially after the immaturity he'd displayed last night.

Jeff was gone by the time I was up and around, but Cal Lindsay looked in to make sure I was all right. Jeff had informed him of Randy's visit and Cal Lindsay was not amused.

"If his pa wasn't so sick I'd go over there and tell him about it. That boy is going to get himself into trouble. He just hasn't got any sense."

"I can certainly agree with that. Did Jeff also tell you of the plans we made for our plantation?"

"Yes'm, he sure did, and they're fine."

"You're as much a part of them as we are, Mr. Lindsay. Papa would have wanted it that way, but even if this was not so, we would insist you remain. Not merely as an employee, but as a partner. We will discuss this later."

"All we have to do is get the farm in condition," he said. "That's not going to be easy, but we'll manage. First thing is to burn the cane. It's rotted by now and the stalks are dry as tinder. If you say so, I'll take care of it when the wind is right. Might not be for a week or two, but when the proper time comes I'll know it."

"You may use your judgment," I said. "I know little of burning the fields."

"Good. Will you be going into the village today?"

"There's certainly no reason to. There's nobody left."

Cal Lindsay nodded. "I got me a key to the general store. Mark Brownlee, who ran it, says we can help ourselves to anything we need and just make a list to be settled for later on."

"You think of everything," I said. "I don't believe I could get along without you."

"Your pa taught me. This is more his doing than mine. I'm just glad you want to keep the farm going. It would have broken his heart if you only wanted to be rid of it."

"Just stay around, Mr. Lindsay, and you'll see how much I wish to be rid of it. We're going to turn out more sugar and syrup and molasses than anybody in Louisiana. And I can't wait to get things started."

It was a quiet day. Jeff had warned me he'd be spending the morning resting after his all-night vigil, and the afternoon in important work connected with his business. Dr. Shea was likely concerned with getting his office ready for moving. Cal Lindsay worked at the sugar house making sure there was no deterioration of equipment.

I found more than enough to do in writing a letter to mama and then trying to understand the books and papers papa had left. I had very little training in business so I had a difficult time and many of the more complicated matters I set aside for Jeff to handle.

I skipped dinner because I was too busy to remember that I was hungry, but at supper I cooked myself a good meal and enjoyed it, even though I was alone. By the time I finished, and I'd begun my impatient wait for Jeff to ap-

pear, it was growing dark. I had accumulated trash which
had to be disposed of and I knew where Yvonne was accustomed to dumping the materials, so I filled a sack and
started out along the path where we'd discovered
Yvonne's body.

As I crossed the spot where we'd found her I repressed
a shudder and kept going. I threw the sack onto a heap of
debris, but hesitated as I turned away. There seemed to be
an animal lying just beyond the garbage heap. I went to it
and discovered it was a red fox, stiff in death. I left it
there, but I intended to tell Mr. Lindsay so he might bury
it.

As I straightened up from my brief examination of the
carcass I heard a wild yell from somewhere in the cane
fields. It came again, a strident and desperate call for help
from a man. This was no false alarm, no ruse to trap me.
No one could have brought out such pathos and terror
without a strong motive for it.

I ran to the edge of the field. The old, dry stalks towered
above my head and I could not see beyond a single row
of them.

"Where are you?" I shouted. "Call out! Tell me where
you are!"

"I can't see! I'm blind! I can't see! I don't know where I
am! Help me! Help me, please!"

I could not afford to delay any longer and run for help.
A man gone blind in the cane field must be in grave danger even if he wasn't frightened to death. I called out again
and began moving through the cane.

The brittle stalks pulled at my dress and frequently in-
flicted scratches deep enough to bleed, but that tragic
voice, growing weaker now, kept me moving. The fields
were vast, covering many arpents of land, and the farm
was composed of a dozen such huge fields. I was sure the
voice came from either the one closest to where I'd first
heard it, or the next one to that and no farther.

"I'm coming!" I shouted. "Keep calling out and stay
where you are! Don't move!"

"I can't see. I can't see anything. What happened? . . ."

The voice was closer now. If only Jeff was with me. Or

Cal Lindsay, or Dr. Shea. To try and find a blind man in this thick growth of plants was almost impossible.

A gray wisp of something coursed between the rows of cane directly in front of me. I thought it to be some kind of ground fog until more of it appeared and I smelled smoke.

I stopped and looked about. It was now almost dark and the crimson glow behind me was all too evident. The cane fields were on fire. I thought Mr. Lindsay must be carrying out our plans, but I put that idea aside. He'd never start a fire at nightfall. That would have been a foolish, almost insane thing to do, and Cal Lindsay was neither foolish nor out of his mind.

I hesitated, torn between the frantic desire to turn back, and the thought of a man gone blind and trapped in the middle of a cane field that would be burning like tinder in the next few minutes.

"Call out!" I shouted. "Call out, please! There isn't much time! The field is on fire! Call out!"

I heard his yell of terror. He too had probably smelled the smoke and had his suspicions confirmed by my shout of fire. I moved on, fighting every foot of the way against the sturdy, tough stalks. Behind me the fire seemed to be gaining, if the glow in the sky had any meaning.

I cried out constantly until my throat grew tired and sore. Finally the smoke became so thick I could no longer call out and I was compelled to keep my mouth shut and to keep from breathing as much as possible.

The blind man was not yet silenced by the thick and acrid smoke. He could still call and guide me. Under ordinary conditions, in a field of pasture land or tall grass, I could have located and reached him in little time, but here I was required to battle my way through the resisting, thick cane.

Then I saw him. The man was stumbling about, crashing into stalks of cane and I could see where he'd fallen several times by the flattened stalks. He kept his face covered with his hands until I reached his side. Then he lowered his hands and I stared into the face of Ed Baker, the village drunk who had accosted and threatened me in the village. His features were contorted by terror. His eyes, wide open, were so red they looked as if they were bathed in blood.

I said, "I'm Carolyn Taylor. I'm alone and I'll try to get you out of here, but we have to hurry. The entire plantation is on fire. The fields are burning and we have to keep ahead of the fire if we can. Don't fight me. Follow where I direct and save your breath. You're going to need it."

"But I can't see. I'm blind. I can't see. Save me! Please save me! I can hear the fire and I can smell the smoke. Save me!"

"Be quiet," I said sharply. "Take my hand. Now move right behind me. Keep going. Don't try to stop for an instant."

I never meant anything so much in my life. The fire, which had been coming up behind us with a savage fury, was now on three sides of us and, I suspected, it would soon be ahead of us as well. If that happened we were finished. No human could plunge through so large an area of flame. Each stalk of cane was like a torch drenched in oil. The heat and smoke were reaching us in proportions that threatened to send us to our knees, gasping for breath and cowering against the heat.

I kept going, half dragging Baker with me. He whimpered and alternately cursed bitterly. I told him to be quiet in no uncertain tones. He subsided, but kept muttering. And how could I blame him? A man suddenly gone blind, finding himself in the middle of an inferno. I stumbled on, watching the fires as they kept closing in. The gap directly ahead was narrowing. In ten minutes or less we'd be surrounded.

The glare and heat were eye searing, the smoke thicker than ever, and I coughed and sought oxygen in desperate gulps of fouled air. I hoped I was headed right. There was no returning in the direction of the mansion. Our only hope was to clear the gap before the fire closed it, and reach the sugar house. That was of brick construction and offered some refuge against the flames. There was nowhere else to go, anyway.

The fire to my left was not fifty feet away, and I could see the fire on my right leaping from row to row and getting closer and closer. I was tempted to let go of Baker because he was slowing me down, but I couldn't. To leave a fellow human in this furnace would have been plain murder.

So I dragged him after me. I didn't even have the breath to encourage him now and he had ceased to make any vocal sounds at all, which was a small blessing. I estimated that in two minutes, three at the most, the fire would close and be all around us. There'd be no escape except to try a suicidal plunge through the flames, and with Baker in tow it would have been impossible. Even alone, I didn't think I could have made it. Behind the flames the stubs of cane were smoldering and throwing off enough heat to sear the skin from a man's body. The only thing to do was keep moving right toward that small and rapidly vanishing gap.

Fire licked at my dress and I had to brush it out with my hand while I kept going. Baker screamed and I looked back to see that his clothes were also afire. But we were clearing the gap. I couldn't stop. I dragged him along until we were beyond the fire and then there was time to push him to the ground and beat out the flames from his clothing.

Once that was accomplished I got him on his feet again. Smoke poured over our heads. The wind had shifted and given the fire more impetus, directing it right behind us. I'd prayed for a chance to stop long enough to get my breath, but we were now compelled to move faster than ever. Fire, in a field of dry cane stalks, can travel faster than a man, with the right breeze, and this fire was being supplied with just that sort of wind. It was also creating an oven of heat within its own boundaries and this also created more wind.

There seemed to be a howling all about me. The heat was beginning to sear, the flames were closer and it was like being pursued by a nightmare from which there would be no awakening.

It was now dark, but darkness had no meaning here, for the flames illuminated everything in bright red. I didn't see the sugar house until I almost ran full tilt into the wall, at a moment when I felt I could go on no longer and that in minutes I would be consumed by the fire. The thick smoke had hidden the structure, but I could place a hand against the already hot wall and follow it until I came to the door.

It was a heavy door and led into the room where the crystallization was done. It would be a strong room, but it might also be a furnace when the fire closed in.

I dragged Baker through, let go of him and he collapsed wordlessly on the floor. I slammed the door shut and shook it to be certain it wouldn't fly open. Then I rubbed soot and smoke out of my eyes and looked about.

I was virtually a stranger here, but I did recall enough to place our location. This was where the advancing wall of fire would hit first. We would know in a matter of moments if we would survive or die. If the fire moved fast enough, the heat inside this room might not generate spontaneous fires that would explode like a bomb. I'd dreaded the speed of the flames, but now I wished they'd be moving so rapidly they'd jump the building.

Baker was groaning. He sat up, but I knew he was unable to see. I had no idea what had happened to his sight and there was no time to ask any questions.

I seized his hand and dragged him to his feet and over to one of the shallow metal crystallization pans. There was water there. There had to be and I found a pump installed in one corner of the room atop a bench. It was in fine working order and I got the cold water flowing. I thrust my head into the stream and for the first time in many minutes I began to feel human and less like some burned-out old log in a fireplace.

I found a pail also, a very large one that looked something like an enormous ladle. I filled this, dragged it across the floor to where Baker sat whimpering and I dumped the contents of the ladle into the shallow pan and told him to lie down in it. I brought more water until he was half covered with water. I threw more on myself. The heat was growing unbearable. Windows had been blown out and tongues of fire seeped into the room from the windows but nothing caught fire. I drenched myself again and poured more water on Baker.

Then it was over. The fire had not leaped the sugar house but it had moved so fast that we endured the maximum effects of the flames for only a minute or two. I sank to the floor, pulled my water-soaked hair back over my head and said a little prayer of thanksgiving.

One thought occurred to me and it made me laugh out loud because it was a mad thought and I was going mad.

I wondered if the bell and whistle aboard the packet were sounding for me and Ed Baker.

THIRTEEN

It began to rain five minutes later. I did what I could to ease Ed Baker's terror and I felt sorry for the man, but he owed me some explanations.

"Can you see the light of the fires?" I asked him.

"Can't see anything. I'm blind. I ain't never going to see again. I know it."

"Perhaps Dr. Shea can help you, or know where you can get help. Now, collect your wits. Tell me how you happened to be in the cane fields on my plantation."

"I didn't know where I was. I had a few drinks and when I woke up I couldn't see. Then the fire started. You're Miss Carolyn, ain't you?"

I'd forgotten he could not see me. "Yes, I'm Carolyn Taylor. You don't remember how you got to the cane field?"

"No, ma'am. I got no idea. I guess you saved my life. I'm beholden. Twice as beholden because I didn't treat you very good. But I was drunk at the time. I swear I ain't never goin' to touch alcohol again. Not one drop."

"That's a fine resolution. It's beginning to rain and that will put out the fires. We're in the sugar house. It's made of brick and it's secure so we're no longer in any danger."

"That's mighty good news."

"We came very close to losing our lives, Mr. Baker."

"Yes'm, reckon we sure did."

"I think the cane fields were set afire deliberately."

"You think somebody was tryin' to kill us?"

"That's exactly what I think. Now, in a short time someone will find us. Before that happens I want you to tell me what you know about the whistle that sounds when someone dies."

His sightless eyes turned toward me. "I don't know anythin', Miss Carolyn. I swear I don't, except I'm scared of that whistle."

"You were one of those who escaped from the packet," I reminded him. "Why should the whistle scare you? For you couldn't possibly have come under the influence of that curse the captain bestowed upon all who he believed would not come to his aid."

"I don't know, but I'm scared. Maybe Cap'n Haley is mad at me too because I didn't get killed."

"Then you believe the captain's ghost is responsible for the bell and the whistle and the deaths?"

"Yes'm, I sure do. Cap'n Haley was a powerful strong man and mighty mad that night at everybody. I believe, all right. He's back. He's been back ever since the first man died under the curse. And he blows the whistle and makes the bell sound because when someone dies it makes the cap'n happy."

I walked away from him and went to one of the empty window frames. Some smoke was drifting in, but the smart breeze which had fanned the flames was gone. The rain was falling moderately hard and the fires were almost out. Some pockets still smoldered, but there were no more leaping flames to light up the night.

Someone was calling my name. I cupped my hands to my mouth and shouted back. An answering hail indicated

I'd been heard. They'd soon guess I must be in the sugar house and come straight to it. I was safe now. So was Ed Baker and I felt sorrier than ever for him. He'd suffered some minor burns and I attempted to treat these with cold water. He grimaced in pain but I'm sure I helped him at least a little.

Cal Lindsay was the first to arrive. He hurried to my side, set down the lantern he carried and worried that I was hurt.

"I'm quite all right," I told him. "Ed Baker needs help. He's gone blind."

"Ed Baker?" Lindsay said in surprise. He hadn't even seen Baker as he came in. Now he went to Baker's side and examined him while he asked him sharp questions in a voice devoid of all compassion. Baker muttered some answers but Cal Lindsay derived no more information from him than I had.

Jeff arrived next, breathless, soaking wet, his face and hands begrimed with ash from the burned cane. In my mind I thought I'd never seen him look more handsome. I was in his arms before he covered ten feet within the sugar house.

"We didn't know you were in the fields," he said. "When the fire started I looked for you and when I couldn't find you . . . and Cal hadn't seen you . . . we guessed you must be in the fields somewhere. I tried to ride a horse into the cane but the animal balked, so Cal and I began searching on foot."

I didn't explain then. We were all so exhausted and so begrimed that we decided to return to the mansion and clean up. There, I bathed and washed the ash out of my hair, wondering while I did so how I had any hair left after the heat of that fire and the sparks which flew about so generously. I dried my hair as much as possible, tied it with a silk ribbon, put on a simple dress and went down to the drawing room, where Cal and Jeff were waiting.

"Ed Baker refused to stay in the house. He's more at home in the stable, I guess," Cal Lindsay explained. "He really is blind, isn't he?"

"Probably the result of drinking bad liquor," Jeff said.

"I hope he gets over it. He certainly didn't have much to say about how he happened to find himself in the cane field."

"I noticed something else," Cal Lindsay said. "Somebody had beaten him up rather severely. There are bruises all over his body. He won't talk about it."

"I wish Dr. Shea would come by," I said. "He must have gone to see Anse Austin tonight and usually he stops off here."

"If he doesn't come in another half hour or so," Jeff said, "I'm going to ride into the village and try to find him. Ed Baker needs a doctor."

"I'm not sure of Baker," Cal Lindsay said. "The fire was started in several places. It was no accident. The fire was deliberately set. Baker was out there in the fields. He could have been wandering about setting the fires. We sure know this was meant to kill you, Miss Carolyn."

I objected to that theory. "He's blind. He'd be killing himself by setting fires that would surely trap him too. And if he was blind, how did he know I was in the fields?"

"He was calling for help, wasn't he?" Cal asked. "That's why you went into the fields. It could have been a trap."

I nodded. "I'd forgotten that. It is true. He drew me into the fields."

"Somebody else could have put Baker out there while he was still dead drunk. Whoever did that would have known Baker would awaken and begin yelling for help. If that person was close by, he'd have seen you go after Baker." Jeff looked at me. "That's when the fires were set. It was a scheme to place you into position so the fire would destroy both you and Baker."

"Am I then under the ill will of the dead Captain Haley?" I asked. "How could he have held me responsible? I was a little girl when the packet grounded and burned. Or do the children of those he cursed come under the threat of being killed?"

Jeff walked over to a window to peer into the night. "I'll give Doc Shea another ten minutes before I go looking for him." He returned to share the sofa with me. "What I'd like to know is where Randy Austin was two hours ago when the fires started. Where Dr. Shea was, and Willie Spencer and, mostly, Hattie. If the fires were started, that person has to be one of those four. There's nobody else left around here."

"Unless Ed Baker set them," Cal said. And then, in a grimmer voice, "Or the idea of a years-old curse is true and Captain Haley has his will after all."

Neither Jeff nor I had any comment to make on that statement. Ten minutes later Jeff decided to go hunting for Dr. Shea, but before he got started we heard a buggy drive up and presently I admitted Dr. Shea. I'd never seen him looking so tired. There were deep circles under his eyes and his face looked drawn. He was in need of a shave as well and he sat down in the drawing room like a man dead tired.

"Anse will likely not last out the night," he said. "He's sinking fast. We saw the fire from Anse's plantation. I came as quickly as I could. Randy insisted I stay there so I'd be on hand when his father died. Otherwise I'd have come at once. As it was, I had to defy him."

"Randy is getting too big a head," Lindsay said. "Coming into the plantation has changed him. He's become very hard to handle."

"He's a mite crazy," Dr. Shea said. "He held a gun on me. And worse than that, he bragged about beating up Ed Baker. For someone like Randy, there's nothing that's more likely to inflate his ego than beating up a man. Even a poor, harmless drunk."

"Ed Baker is here," I said. "He's blind."

Dr. Shea arose wearily. "Where is he? I'd better look at him right now."

"He's all right," Cal Lindsay said. "He's down at the stable. So it was Randy who beat him up. I wondered. Ed wouldn't say a word."

"How does it happen he's here?" Dr. Shea asked. "If he's blind how did he find his way here?"

"I heard him calling for help in the cane fields," I explained. "When I went after him, someone else set half a dozen fires that almost killed me and Baker."

"What's Ed got to say about it?" Dr. Shea asked.

"He doesn't even know how he got into the cane fields," I said. "I do think it might be wise to examine him. Perhaps his eyesight isn't gone completely."

Dr. Shea said, "Cal, come along with me and give me a hand with him. Sometimes he's not willing to submit to an examination and I'll need you to hold him down."

"I'll go," Cal said, "but I don't think he'll have to be held down this time. He's not in very good condition."

They hurried down to the stable. Jeff seemed to be deep in thought. I moved closer to him and touched his cheek, bristly with beard stubble.

"I want you to know this," he said. "I don't trust anybody. From here on I'm not sharing my suspicions with anyone except you. And I'm not waiting for Anse to die. I'm not waiting for anything. I intend to find out who could have set those fires."

"Dr. Shea was at the Austin plantation," I said. "And he says Randy was there."

"He didn't say when. He could have set the fires, driven fast to the Austin place and been there when the fires were first seen. Or Randy could have set the fires and reached his place before Shea arrived. But leave those two out of it. Where was Hattie and where was Willie Spencer?"

"It's not going to be easy to find out where those two people were. They stay so much by themselves you'd have to take their word for it."

"Maybe. Soon as Dr. Shea leaves I'm going to pay Willie Spencer a visit and then I'm going to call on Hattie. If she aims a gun at me I'll take it away from her. Time somebody did anyway. One of these days she'll open fire."

"I'm going with you," I told him. "I don't want to be in this house alone again."

"You won't be. I'll see to that. We're going to find out what's back of all this attempted murder, these deaths which are so completely unexplained. And some people are not going to be permitted to live like hermits and not account for their actions any longer."

"Look at what's happened," I agreed with him. "So many people have died. An entire village depopulated, ruined. Not three hours ago I almost lost my life. We either have to settle this at once or clear out. If there is such a thing as a dead man's curse and phantoms who ring bells and blow whistles where there is no whistle and only a bell that cannot be rung, then we can't fight them."

"Dead men's curses do not exist. Whistles are only sounded when there is steam to sound them and bells ring only when there are clappers that move. A human being is responsible for what has happened and we're going to find him."

"But where do we start?" I asked.

"First of all, we will trust no one except Cal. He'll be of great help. We'll begin with Willie Spencer. His cabin is closest to the plantation. From there we go to visit Hattie and, if we don't wind up being shot, we'll go on to call on Randy Austin. If nothing develops by then, we'll keep on until something does."

"I have a feeling," I said, "that someone is watching me at times. Perhaps I should pretend that I've retired for the night while you are close by for my protection."

"A good idea. I'll speak to Cal when I can get him alone, and tell him to patrol the outside of the house as if we were inside. That will perfect the illusion."

I nestled against his shoulder. I was tired of death, mysterious whistles, impending disaster and angry people. Jeff must have guessed this too.

"What a wonderful place this used to be," he said. "The plantation, the village, the people, the sugar house going full blast. The dock piled high with sacks of sugar and barrels of syrup. The riverboats coming in with their calliopes going, passengers lining the rails. It will be that way again. I'd welcome the sound of the packet whistles coming in on the wind and having no other meaning than to announce the arrival or the departure of the ship."

"I like everything you said except the sound of the whistle. That will never have a cheerful meaning for me again, Jeff. It will only remind me of what happened here.

"I know, but even that memory will fade with the years."

"If they are spent with you, darling, I'm sure it will. I want to stay here. I want to run the plantation. And just think of it, a few months ago I was set against coming here, even though I knew papa was so ill. I was going to miss the opera and the balls and the dinners . . . everything that represented my life in New Orleans. Now it seems like something so distant in the past I have a hard time remembering."

"You shall have both, the plantation and the life in New Orleans," Jeff promised.

Dr. Shea arrived, blew out the lantern he was carrying and set it on the porch. Then he joined us.

"Ed Baker didn't leave the village with the rest of them. He stayed behind because he thought he could raid Oliver Talbot's tavern. But it seems Oliver had few intentions of coming back and took all his supply of alcoholic beverages with him except a keg of whiskey which he'd had for years and was of such bad quality that he never served it. In my opinion that keg contained whiskey in which dangerous poisons were somehow introduced. Ed Baker drank himself into a stupor with the stuff and it made him go blind. I don't know if he'll ever have his sight returned. I doubt it, but I didn't tell him this."

"How badly was he beaten?" Jeff asked.

"Quite badly. I can't figure out if he was beaten just before he wound up in the cane fields, or if it occurred before he got drunk. Randy admits he was staggering and crazy when he drove him off his plantation."

"What was he doing there?" I asked.

"He claimed he wanted to pay Anse Austin a visit before Anse died. That's what set Randy off. His father near death and this drunken idiot coming to call."

"Could Baker tell you how he got in the cane field?" I asked.

"He has no recollection of how he got there, but I surmise that after Randy beat him into near unconsciousness, Baker somehow stumbled away from the Austin plantation, managed to make it to this one and wandered into the cane fields without really knowing where he was going or what he was doing. It might even be that he thought he was in the cane fields at the Austin plantation and he set the fires in revenge for the beating."

"Will you take care of him?" Jeff asked. "He may need more medical attention. We can question him at length later on."

"Yes, I'll bring him to my office and let him stay there. I'll also be able to determine if he'll ever see again. I can certainly devote a lot of time to this examination and treatment. He's the only patient I've got other than Anse Austin, and poor Anse will not last much longer."

"Thank you," I said. "If he wasn't blind or injured I'd agree to keep him here, but I'm sure he does need your services, Doctor."

"He'll be all right. I'll collect him now and be on my way. I'll let you know when Anse goes. Probably before morning. I'll go back there within the next couple of hours. And stay until . . . there's no longer any reason to stay."

Jeff and I walked down to the stable while Dr. Shea drove his buggy there. By the time we arrived, he and Cal had helped Ed Baker into the buggy and Dr. Shea drove him away. We watched them disappear into the night.

Jeff said, "Cal, we're not waiting for Anse to die. We're going to visit people we suspect. Because we may be watched, we'll slip out of the house after Carolyn pretends to go to bed and I take up a position downstairs. To make it seem even more real I want you to patrol the outside of the estate. Don't leave it unless something happens."

"Like the whistle sounding and the bell ringing?" Cal asked.

"Exactly. Then come running."

"Count on me," Cal said.

"We'll wait a reasonable length of time and then slip out the back door," I said. "I'll have fresh lanterns ready. We may need them."

Half an hour later I blew out the lamps, except for the one I carried. I went upstairs to my room and moved about so that my shadow could be seen through the window shades. Finally, I blew out the last lamp, waited a few minutes and then made my way through the darkened house to the kitchen and the back door. It was an eerie experience. One I didn't care for, but I regained my courage when Jeff met me just outside the rear door. I handed him one of the lanterns not yet lit, and we made our way through a ground fog just coming up. The air was sultry and very humid. I didn't know the way, so I let Jeff take the lead and he brought me to within a few yards of the small, one-room cabin where Willie Spencer lived. The cabin was in darkness.

We now lit our lanterns and then boldly approached. Jeff knocked on the door, but there was no reply. We were ready to enter the cabin anyway when we heard Willie coming. He was moving slowly, like a man in pain.

He came to a dead stop when he saw our lanterns. Jeff called his name and Willie continued approaching until he confronted us.

"Good evening," he said. "You'll have to excuse me. I must get inside and tend to these burns. I was trapped in the cane-field fire. My legs, arms and, I think, my face—"

"The fire was out sometime ago," I said.

"I know that. I walked to the village to have Dr. Shea help me but he wasn't there. Neither was anyone else, so I came back here."

"How did it happen that you went into the cane fields when they were burning?" Jeff asked.

"I heard someone calling. I had to respond. I happened to be close by so I went looking for the man. I never found him. I suppose the poor devil was burned to death."

"If the man you heard was Ed Baker," I said, "he's all right now except that he's blind. That was not connected with the fire, but it was he who called for help. I went to his aid also."

"Ed Baker blind? Where is he? If there is anything I can do to help the poor fellow. . . ."

"He's under Dr. Shea's care. The doctor was at the Austin place. That's why you couldn't find him."

"Austin is still alive, then?"

"Last we heard he was, but Dr. Shea said he can't last much longer."

"It's a wonder he's still alive. Please come in."

He opened the door, entered first and lit lamps. Now I saw that he was burned in several places. He produced some butter from his ice box and I helped him cover the burned areas with this. I applied bandage made from strips of bed sheets I cut with scissors. By the time I finished, Willie said he felt better.

"We're going to call on Hattie," I informed him. "She'll likely take a gun to us but she's got to listen. We need information. She may be able to help. Hattie didn't come to this village by plain chance. Otherwise she wouldn't make it a point to be at every funeral of a man whose death was saluted with the ghostly whistle."

"I'll go with you," Willie offered.

"But those burns . . . the way you must feel. . . ." I objected, but not strenuously. Hattie was far more apt to accept him than either Jeff or me.

"I'm quite all right. The pain is not as severe now, thanks to your help. What do you wish to know from Hattie?"

"Do you think she'll talk to you?" Jeff asked.

"Yes, I'm sure she will. I've talked to her before and she trusts me. Shall we go now?"

Willie seemed astonishingly strong for what he'd been through, and he led the way to Hattie's cabin at a rapid pace which even Jeff found hard to keep up with and which left me panting. While neither Jeff nor I had a chance to discuss Willie's strange presence at the scene of the fire, I had a feeling that he was telling the truth. At any rate, there was no way we could prove he was not.

Hattie's cabin was in darkness. Jeff seized my hand and brought me to a halt. "Remember, she has a gun," he warned. "Willie, are you sure she won't start shooting at you?"

"Not if she knows who I am. You two stay here."

Willie moved on. He began calling Hattie's name as he drew closer and closer to the cabin. He identified himself a dozen times, but there was no answer. He swung the lantern in a signal for us to join him. When we did he opened the cabin door and we went inside.

There was barely room for the three of us. The cabin was packed with furniture and the interior was completely out of keeping with the seedy-looking exterior. Whoever Hattie was, she was not poverty stricken. This was quality furniture. A small bed, neatly covered with a silken spread. A small sofa and two overstuffed chairs. A fireplace of fieldstone looked as if it was used often and over a long period of time. There was a pantry and kitchen, both well furnished and stocked. The cabin walls were all but papered with framed paintings, some of them very good. On the two tables was an assortment of bric-a-brac. I picked up a Dresden statuette of a doll, exquisitely done and obviously valuable.

"Well, she's not here, that's certain," Jeff said. "Maybe we should look around outside."

"I wouldn't disturb anything in the cabin," Willie said. "I knew it was a neat and well-furnished place, but not quite like this."

We went around to the back of the place. A good-sized shed drew our attention, for the door was wide open. There was a stable beside it and this too was open.

"Hattie kept a horse," Willie explained. "I don't know why she kept it. She did no farming and therefore no plowing. She has a buggy. Or she did have . . . yes . . . it's in the stable."

"But there's no horse," Jeff commented. "I don't think Hattie rides a saddle horse."

"I don't think so either. Maybe she got rid of the horse. Perhaps it died. It was a rather old animal the last time I saw it and that was a year ago."

Jeff tilted his lantern and then knelt on the ground before the shed. "No, the horse must be all right. Some sort of vehicle was driven out of the shed not too long ago. I can see the tracks plainly because the short spell of rain made enough mud to create visible tracks."

"I never knew she had another vehicle," Willie said.

"She must have," Jeff said. "I have an idea there are a lot of things you don't know about her, Willie."

"I think we should wait here until she returns." I offered my advice for what it was worth. "That way we can catch her when she's not within reach of her rifle."

"A good idea," Jeff said. "The rifle is in the cabin. I saw it leaning against the wall. Hattie has some explaining to do and we'd better see that she does it the moment she comes back."

"Then we'd best move into the shadow and blow out our lanterns so she won't be warned and run away," Willie suggested.

We did extinguish the lanterns and we took up a position close enough to the cabin to intercept her and block any attempt on her part to run away. We grew silent as we waited. I judged it must have been thirty minutes at least and I was growing restive with this inaction and suspense.

Then it came. Not one of us had given any thought to the fact that Anse Austin was dying, that Dr. Shea was with him to do what he could, and that when Anse died the whistle would sound and the ship's bell would toll.

I had never before experienced such a wave of terror as that which the sound of the whistle brought to me. It came on a mild wind and it seemed to grow louder and louder, even though I knew that was an illusion. The ship's bell sounded but briefly. The whistle kept up its doleful, dreadful howl.

It meant but one thing. Another man had died.

FOURTEEN

Since we had walked to Willie Spencer's cabin and then to Hattie's, we had to hurry to the packet on foot. As we neared it we met Cal who took only time to wave as he ran on ahead while Jeff and I maintained a slower pace. I knew this was because of me, but I didn't object. At that moment I wanted nothing any more than Jeff's company. The echoes of that ghostly whistle still rang in my ears and I was as terrorized as I had been when the whistle first sounded after my arrival at the plantation.

Jeff led me through a thick forest growth, along a narrow path which, he told me, was a shortcut. My ankle was throbbing again. When we came out of this darkness which had been lit only with our lanterns, I saw the knoll rising above us and atop it the grim skeleton of a ship which had died years ago.

"Anse must be dead," I said, when I'd regained my breath sufficiently so that I could speak.

"Yes, no doubt of that. I'm going aboard again. Want to come along?"

"I don't want to stay here, or anywhere else, alone. Jeff, I'm terribly frightened. That . . . whatever it is . . . keeps killing people and we can do nothing because we don't know how to cope with this situation. We may be next."

"I won't leave you. And I have a feeling we're getting closer and closer to the truth behind this ghost, or whatever it is." He took my hand. "I'm sure we won't find anything aboard the ship, but let's look anyway."

We walked across the sagging gangplank. Jeff examined the deck for any fresh signs that his sprinkling of dust had been disturbed, but the recent rain had washed most of it away. We entered the salon and examined it and some of the cabins where the dust was intact. Nobody had been here since our last visit. On the hurricane deck we discovered no trace of an intruder and no signs of anybody having been there. The whistle was still a decayed, eroded column of useless metal.

"Someone is on the little road below the ship," Jeff observed. "Must be Cal. Let's go see."

"There's certainly nothing on this old hulk," I said.

"Never has been, in my opinion, but maybe Cal has something."

Again we crossed the gangplank, but this time we scrambled down the slope at the back of the ship. Cal signaled us with his lantern and when we joined him he quickly led us to the rutted, narrow lane which began at the main road to the village and ended right here where the ship had foundered.

"This road leads nowhere," Cal said. "It's not even a road, just a trail. It was used to haul everything heavy but movable off the ship after it was abandoned. There wasn't any looting. Folks were afraid to go aboard. So if a wagon was driven to this point, it must have been driven by someone who wanted to visit the ship. Look . . . here . . . it rained and the dirt is still wet and muddy. See the wagon tracks? Not a buggy or carriage, but a wagon and a heavy one. Unless it was carrying something extra heavy."

"One more thing," Jeff looked up from where he knelt in the dirt. "These seem to be the same kind of tracks we saw leading to and from the shed behind Hattie's cabin."

We told Cal what we had found in our visit to Hattie's. The connection didn't surprise him but rather confirmed suspicions of his own.

"I'm for going back to Hattie's place right now," he said.

I said, "It would be easier if we returned to the mansion first and hitched up a carriage. We'll want to go to Anse Austin's place too."

"I'll go on ahead," Cal said. "I'll have a carriage ready by the time you get there."

I was near the point of exhaustion and thoughts of making my way through that long forest trail by lantern light dismayed me so much I felt I could not go through with it.

"Please," I said. "We're not far from Anse Austin's place and it's on our way back to the plantation house, so why not find out if the whistle was for Anse. Then we can return to Hattie's place."

"I don't see why not," Jeff agreed. "If Hattie's is hiding something in that shed behind her cabin, she has no idea we suspect she is. It can wait."

"I'm not so sure," Cal disagreed. "Why not let me go back there alone while you two see about Anse? We'll meet at the plantation house."

"Good idea," Jeff approved. "Watch out for Hattie and that rifle she keeps handy."

Cal nodded, somewhat grimly, I thought, and began hurrying toward the forest trail. Jeff and I walked slowly, out of deference to my state of exhaustion.

"You haven't recovered fully from that experience in the burning cane fields," Jeff said. "No wonder you're tired. We'll make this visit as brief as possible and then head for home."

When we reached the Austin house we knew Anse was dead, for the house was brilliantly lighted from top to bottom. Dr. Shea's buggy was out front. Randy let us in. I wasn't certain whether he was really as sad as he pretended to be, or whether he was trying hard to hide his delight in now being the owner of this plantation.

"Pa's dead," he said. "You heard the whistle, I suppose?"

"We heard it," Jeff said. "Is Dr. Shea upstairs?"

"Yes. He was there when pa died. Mama is broken up pretty much. We're going to take papa's body to Williston because mama says she doesn't want him buried in this terrible town. I don't blame her any, but I don't see what the difference is when you think about it."

I hurried upstairs. Dr. Shea was in the bedroom where Anse's body still lay. I nodded as I passed by the door and indicated I would see him later. Marie Austin was in another of the bedrooms, sitting by a window. There was a sodden handkerchief in her hand and her eyes were red from weeping. I went to her at once and kissed her cheek before I drew up a chair and sat beside her.

"What is this awful thing that kills good men?" she asked me. "Poor Anse, lying there wondering if the whistle was going to blow before he died or afterward. I'm leaving this place forever and I'm taking Anse's body with me for burial somewhere else. This whole area is cursed."

"I don't believe that," I said. "But I can't blame you for going away, just as my mother did. I'm sure Randy will stay and take care of things until someone finds out what's really behind all these deaths."

"What's behind it?" She stared at me. "You know what's behind it. Nobody profits from these deaths. There's only one reason: the spirit of the captain who cursed every-one. There is no reason for killing all those people except out of revenge, and only a ghost could cause the packet whistle to blow and its bell to ring."

"Yes," I said, mainly to mollify her, "I have to agree with you about the whistle and the bell. Nothing human could make them sound for any reason."

"I sent for the undertaker," she said. "I'm going to have him take Anse to Williston. I'm going to ride behind the hearse all the way. Randy is going with me and I swear I won't be back."

"We'll look out for your house and your stock while Randy is gone," I promised. "I've got to go now. I'm truly sorry, Mrs. Austin, and I pray this is the last time the whistle will ever blow."

She nodded and lowered her head as I left. Dr. Shea met me in the hall. "She's badly affected," he said, "and leaving here is the best medicine for her. I'm leaving too. If you'll take my advice, you and Jeff ought to go away as well. A man can take so much and then he can't bear up any longer. Watching poor Anse die without being able to do a thing for him. It makes me out a poor doctor."

"You're a fine doctor," I said. "No one could have saved those people. You did your very best."

"I suppose so," he said in a voice utterly lacking in spirit. "Is Jeff with you?"

"Yes, he's downstairs talking to Randy."

"Where's Cal?"

"He's gone to see about Hattie," I replied. I regretted having made that admission as soon as I finished speaking.

"What about Hattie?" he demanded.

"Oh, Cal is just checking up on everyone."

"What's he done about Willie Spencer, then?"

"Willie was with us when the whistle sounded."

"I see. Are you and Jeff going to leave?"

"I don't know. I doubt it, but honestly, I am so fright-ened. And there's nobody left in the village. Now the Austin farm will be deserted for some time. I don't know what I'm going to do."

"I'll be leaving right after the Austins do. I'll take Ed

Baker along. He's still unable to see. Maybe he'll never see again. I can't leave him here."

"That's to your credit," I said. "I'm sure we'll see you again before long, but I do wish you all the good fortune in the world in getting your new practice going."

"Thank you. It's not going to be easy, but I'll manage. I won't go down to see Jeff now. Mrs. Austin needs someone with her as much as possible. Good-bye, Carolyn. I wish things could have been different. I'm sure I will never forget how much I've been in love with you."

I left him then and went downstairs where Jeff and Randy were talking earnestly. Jeff realized that I wished to leave and go home to rest, so he arose immediately.

"Randy will be back within a week," Jeff told me. "I've promised to look in on the place while he's away and take care of the horses."

"I told your mother the same thing, Randy," I said.

"I'll get back sooner than that if I can," Randy said. "I ain't scared of that whistle. This is my plantation now and I'm going to run it big."

"I have no doubt of that," I said. "Good-bye, Randy. You have my sympathy over the death of your father."

Moments later Jeff and I were walking back to my own house. It was a considerable distance, but far shorter than a side trip to Hattie's cabin. The mansion loomed ghostly and forbidding in the night. There were no lights lit, of course, and the place seemed to be composed of more shadows than substance. We looked for any signs of Cal Lindsay having reached the house ahead of us, but he was nowhere to be found.

Jeff lit all the lamps in the drawing room and also those in the dining room. I wasn't hungry, but I knew Jeff must be, so we settled down in the kitchen while I made coffee and found both ham and chicken in the ice box. Poor Yvonne had made bread before she died and I used it to make sandwiches. Jeff and I talked across the kitchen table while we ate.

"Let's say that the whistle and the bell are sounded by a human being and not a ghost," Jeff said. "Now, the whole village has cleared out, so we can't really suspect anybody who used to live there. We have left: Dr. Shea, Randy, Hattie, Ed Baker, Willie Spencer and Cal Lindsay. At the time the whistle blew tonight, Dr. Shea and Randy were both at the bedside of Randy's father. Cal was with us and so was Willie Spencer, up to a point. Ed Baker is blind and we can eliminate him. Who does that leave? Hattie! There's nobody else."

"If that's true then Hattie must have had someone she loved very much aboard the packet."

"True enough. She didn't arrive in town until some time after the tragedy—three or four years, I think. But it was after she got here that the deaths began to happen. If she is guilty, the curse issued by Captain Haley had no meaning or substance. Hattie merely took advantage of it."

"How did she manage to kill all those people?" I asked.

"She didn't impress me as being an unusual woman in any way. To have planned and carried out so many murders required skill and great intelligence. Maybe she has both, but I still don't see how she could accomplish it."

"We're going to find out," Jeff promised. "Cal should be back soon and he'll have found Hattie if she's still around."

Half an hour went by and Cal hadn't returned from Hattie's place. I was growing worried and Jeff even more so. After we left the kitchen he paced up and down nervously, going to a window every few minutes to peer out into the night.

I said, "Jeff, I think you'd best harness the carriage and we'll go looking for Cal. We've waited long enough."

"That's what I've been thinking. I'll be right back."

Alone in the big house, my nervousness increased, but Jeff was back before it really affected me too much. I hurried out to get aboard the carriage and we were on our way to Hattie's place.

We were within a quarter of a mile of it when Jeff pulled up quickly. Ahead of us someone was signaling with a lantern. Jeff waited while the man approached us and I knew if it was someone we didn't trust, or someone intent on doing us harm, Jeff would have the carriage moving in time to get away safely. But it was Cal Lindsay and I exhaled slowly in great relief.

"Get down off there," he said. "Hattie's loose somewhere in these woods and she's pretty handy with that rifle. I looked for the gun when I got back to her cabin, but it was gone and so was Hattie."

Jeff and I were out of the carriage promptly, and with Cal we hurried to the brush where we would not be easily seen. Cal was bursting with something important to tell us, but first he made certain we were not being stalked. We remained very quiet for several minutes while we listened for the sounds of someone nearby. When we were certain we were not being approached, Cal told us what he'd found.

"The ghost!" he said. "I found the ghost! I think you should see it before I tell you what it is. We'll have to risk going to Hattie's place, but I doubt she'll be anywhere around there because I led her on a wild-goose chase to get her as far away from the cabin as possible. Are you both willing to take a chance?"

"I am," I said. "I can't imagine how you found a ghost."

"It's a big one, all paint and glitter. Come on. It's not far from here."

We moved through the forest, following Cal who knew his way about well. When we came into view of the cabin and the shed and stable, we crouched down to observe the place for several minutes. Cal then signaled we were to remain where we were while he went on to make sure we were not walking into some kind of a trap. We didn't speak and every move we made was done as silently as possible.

My nerves were on edge again and I could hear the beat of my heart as the tension grew. We lost sight of Cal, for he was moving forward, bent over and sometimes on all fours. He'd carried his lantern, unlighted as ours were, so when we saw his lantern, now lit, swinging in a signal, we knew Cal estimated that we were safe enough.

We hurried to the stable where he waited for us. "The horse is in there." He pulled open the stable door and we could see a sleek, fat horse in its stall. "That horse has been working not long ago. Hattie didn't take time to rub him down. Now I'll show you what the horse was pulling. I'll show you the ghost that blows whistles and rings bells. And why I never thought of it before beats me."

He pulled open the door to the shed and held his lantern high. Jeff and I gazed in considerable awe at a calliope. A large one, mounted on the bed of a heavy wagon. It was painted red with gold trim and it looked like a church organ, redecorated and misplaced. Jeff clambered onto the wagon and examined the instrument. He placed his hand on the steam box and quickly withdrew it.

"Been used not long ago."

"Sure it was," Cal said. "One of the notes this thing produces must sound like a packet whistle. And there's an old ship's bell here too. There's your ghost!"

"Hattie!" Jeff jumped down from the wagon. "She found out when someone was about to die and drove this thing out to the lane behind the knoll where the packet rests. She got up steam, blew the whistle and sounded the bell and then headed back to her cabin. She could make it in ten minutes and if anybody came along the road, she could drive off into the woods and never be seen."

"That calliope," Cal said, "came off the packet. I know it had one. Most of 'em do, but who'd associate a calliope with a ship's whistle? Nobody thought of it."

"Hattie couldn't have gotten that thing off the packet alone," I said.

"She must have had help," Jeff agreed. "But it was removed years ago and whoever got it off the ship for Hattie never realized what it was going to be used for. No doubt she chose somebody who'd not be staying around long."

"She planned all this for years," Cal said. "She's not far away, I'll bet. We'll have to be mighty careful because she's got that rifle and, I imagine, plenty of ammunition."

"In spite of that," Jeff said, "we have to go back to her cabin and search for anything that will tell us who she is. Before she beats us to it and destroys everything."

"Then let's go there now," I said. An hour ago I'd been so tired I didn't know how I could go on, but this significant find, the disclosure that the whistle we'd heard with such ominous meaning was nothing more than a gaudy calliope, had made me forget my weariness.

"We'd better hurry," Jeff said.

We headed back toward Hattie's cabin, this time with lanterns swinging. Cal, who was leading us, broke into the clearing at the road where we'd left the carriage. He'd no sooner moved from the protection of the brush than a shot whistled within a foot of his head.

Cal whirled about and leaped head first into the brush. He scurried toward us and signaled for quiet. When he spoke, it was in a whisper.

"I should have known that's where she'd wait. At the carriage, because she knew we'd go back past it. We've got to reach the cabin and we've got to keep from getting shot. I've no gun with me, nor have you, I suppose."

"I'm unarmed," Jeff admitted. "I have a suggestion. You and I, Cal, will move away from this spot and head toward the cabin. But we'll make some noise. Not enough to indicate it's on purpose, but if we're lucky we'll draw her away and Carolyn can get to the carriage and drive home before Hattie knows what's happened."

"I'm going with you," I said indignantly. "This is as much my fight as yours."

Jeff grasped me by the shoulders. "Darling, you'll be doing more than your part. Once at the house, you can get rifles and ammunition ready. One of us will be back for them."

"There are rifles in my room above the stable," Cal told me. "Lots of bullets too. Bring them to the house and be sure to load both guns. Keep them handy and if anybody comes, use them if necessary. We may not be able to fool Hattie."

"I can tell you one thing," Jeff added. "No matter what Dr. Shea says, Hattie is not crazy. She couldn't be and have done what she's accomplished. I think she's a very sly, intelligent woman bent on murder for revenge. That makes her very dangerous because we have no idea who she'll turn on next."

I could see the wisdom of my not wandering around in

the night, adding to the problems of these two men and only exposing myself, and them as well, to Hattie's rifle fire.

"I'll go back," I said. "Please be careful, both of you."

"As our lives depend on it," Jeff said, "you can be sure we will be. Now stay right here. Give us at least ten minutes and when you start for the carriage, do so in a manner that keeps the carriage between you and the other side of the road, because that's where Hattie seems to be. I hope we'll be able to draw her away. You'll be taking a big chance, darling. If you reach the carriage, get out of here as fast as you can. If you're fired upon, head back to the brush and wait for us."

Our whispered conversation at an end, I sat down on an old log to wait. Jeff went off in one direction, Cal in another. Presently I heard them moving. Small sounds like a dry branch being trampled underfoot or a bush being brushed aside to permit passage. Normal sounds which would give away the general area of their location, but not arouse any suspicion this was only a ruse to draw Hattie away.

I had no means of telling how much time had passed but when I judged about ten minutes had gone by, I ventured into the clearing beside the road. Nothing happened. The horse was placidly waiting and not at all nervous as horses would be if someone lurked close by.

I got onto the seat, picked up the reins and slapped the horse gently with them. The carriage moved. I made a clumsy turn which took a long time, but no shots were fired at me and I began to feel safer.

Once the carriage was headed back, I prodded the horse to its fullest speed. My ankle was beginning to ache again. It had been sore all this time but now it was throbbing because I'd been on it so long and I'd tramped over several miles of uneven ground.

I reached the mansion and drove straight down to the stable. I hurried up to the loft where Cal Lindsay lived. There I quickly found a shotgun and a rifle. I also discovered the boxes of ammunition. I sat down and loaded both barrels of the shotgun, filled the ammunition chamber of the rifle, and only then did I leave the loft and head back to the house. I let myself in. I had, of course, darkened my lantern long ago and I left it in the carriage. When I was safely inside the house I decided not to betray my presence by lighting any lamps. If Hattie had been here and seen the place dark, she'd surely return with murderous intent if she saw lights in the windows now.

I placed the guns across a chair in the reception hall before I moved into the drawing room, where I pulled a chair up to one of the windows and sat down to wait for Jeff and Cal to return.

Until now there hadn't been time to feel that creepy, crawling fear which began to possess me now. The interior of this darkened mansion, where two people I loved had so recently died, was not an atmosphere which calmed me. Lack of sleep, a throbbing ankle and exhaustion all combined to bring me close to tears. All I could do was sit there in the window, hoping to see Jeff or Cal returning, while I listened for sounds within the mansion. And there were many because these great, old houses seemed to possess a noisy life of their own in the stillness of the night.

FIFTEEN

Gradually I grew accustomed to the night sounds and my fears slowly began to leave me. Here, in this darkness and silence, I found I was able to think more clearly than at any time since I'd arrived at the plantation.

I wondered how a woman like Hattie had carried out all these murders. How she ever planned this and gotten the inspiration to use a calliope to substitute for the packet whistle.

When I'd seen her at the cemetery she'd seemed to be more like a simpering, foolish old woman rather than someone who schemed so cleverly. And my encounter with her when she aimed a gun at me was not what I would call any display of unusual intelligence on her part.

Also, how had she lived all these years alone, friendless, and yet able to maintain a small, but extremely comfortable—and costly—household, even if it consisted of but two rooms in a cabin? Most of all, how did she manage to reach her victims? How had she known when they were about to die?

Only one person, except for the immediate family, would have known the time of death and that was Dr. Shea. I thought back. He'd been in practice here before the first victim of the so-called Captain Haley's curse was struck down.

True, Hattie had attended all the funerals, save that of Yvonne. Dressing in white and simpering at the rear of the mourners did signify she was getting a measure of grim pleasure out of the graveside rites. Of course, someone she loved must have died aboard the packet. That might be determined later, but there were more important questions and they involved Dr. Shea.

Why had Yvonne been killed, and how? I tried to visualize what her final moments must have been like. She'd gone out to dispose of trash in the dump where she threw waste matter. She'd not been carrying any of this when we found her, which meant she'd been to the dump and was returning to the house.

All along I'd suspected that the victims of this evil scheming had been somehow poisoned by the use of something that was too subtle to be detected which had somehow been administered over a period of time to cause the victim to die gradually. Whoever managed this was trying to draw all the drama possible out of it. Causing the entire village to worry, bringing to the men whom Captain Haley had cursed that night the constant threat of death. The next victim didn't know it until he was stricken and then there began the wait for the whistle to announce another victory for the ghost of Captain Haley.

Quite suddenly an idea came to me. If all these victims were poisoned, who could have administered poison without detection? Dr. Shea alone could have done this, possibly increasing the dosage over a period of time and then providing a massive dose which would be fatal.

I called myself an idiot for entertaining such an idea. Dr. Shea was a fine man, a capable doctor and trusted by everyone. I'd be a fool to even suggest what I'd been thinking to anybody else. Dr. Shea had shown nothing but kindness and a genuine desire to help those afflicted. Besides, what did he have to do with the packet and its passengers?

I peered out into the night, but there were no signs of either Jeff or Cal and I was relieved not to see some shadowy figure, carrying a rifle, moving about in the dark.

I wondered, rather idly at the moment, what had happened to the bottle of medicine which Dr. Shea had given papa. I was back on that track again and I tried to thrust the suspicion out of my mind. I decided that I'd look for the medicine bottle and if I found it, I could then easily dismiss all this unwarranted suspicion against a man I admired.

Now I had to light a lamp, and carrying it, I went upstairs to papa's room. I opened the door and stepped inside. Yvonne had cleaned it thoroughly. There was no bottle on the table beside the bed. I looked in the bathroom and found no trace of the medicine. So, it was time to drop this suspicion forever.

But somewhere in my memory lay a dim scene from the past of Yvonne working in papa's room right after he'd died. She had picked up the bottle of medicine and thrust it into the pocket of her apron. I was sure I'd seen her do that.

Now, at least mildly excited, I hurried to Yvonne's room and went through it carefully. There was no medicine bottle. Yvonne would not have kept it around anyway. She had been one of the neatest persons I'd ever known, allowing no useless objects to accumulate. So she would have disposed of the bottle. She'd have taken it, along with other refuse, I supposed, to the dump, far at the rear of the house.

I gasped aloud. I hadn't seen the bottle there, but I had seen a dead fox. An animal that had no doubt prowled the collection of refuse looking for something to eat. If the cork had slipped from the bottle and its contents poured out on something the fox had eaten . . . .

I ran downstairs, through the house and into the kitchen, where I lit a lantern. I was now thoroughly excited and alarmed. I ran along the path, the lantern swinging at my side. I reached the dump and now there were two dead animals lying just beyond it. I bent, searching the small mounds of rubbish, and I came upon the bottle of medicine. The cork was not sealing the bottle, but lay to one side and the contents—the medicine papa had taken so faithfully—had flowed out to mix with bits of food.

Dr. Shea! I straightened up and I shuddered because I, among many others, must have been on the edge of death all the time when Dr. Shea was ministering to us. He'd arrived in town just before the first death. He'd attended every victim. He would have known, within a few hours, when the next patient would die from taking the final dose of the medicine, probably made especially lethal to insure death when Dr. Shea wished it to occur.

He would have told Hattie. There must be some connection between them. I turned and fled back to the stable where I'd left the carriage. The horse was moving nervously, but my mind was not on signs of someone being hidden nearby. I thought only of reaching Jeff and Cal as quickly as I could with this alarming news.

Of course, I might have been wrong and accusing a fine man without enough evidence, but too many things fell snugly into place. No one else could have planned and carried out all these murders and kept the real reason for death from anyone. He'd claimed he'd sent parts of the body for laboratory work but nobody ever tried to find out if he really did. He was a respected man, trusted and believed scrupulously honest. I'd been fooled as much as anyone else, perhaps more so because there had been a few moments when I'd genuinely wondered if I might be in love with him.

I reached the carriage and began to get into it. There was a flurry of steps behind me. Before I could turn I was seized by one arm and yanked off the carriage step.

Dr. Shea seized me in a strong grip. His face was quite impassive but his voice was edged with anger, even though it was modulated and low.

"Poor Carolyn," he said. "I dreaded the moment you'd stumble onto the truth. Why did you have to be so inquisitive? Why didn't you leave here when your mother did?"

"You must be mad," I said. "Doctor, you must be totally mad."

"Oh no, not mad. I knew what I was doing all the time and I only wish there'd be more opportunities to kill some of the others who were too cowardly to help my father that night."

"Captain Haley was your father?" I asked in complete surprise.

"I thought you'd certainly guessed that. Yes, he was my father. He died when there was no reason why he should. My mother swore she would avenge his death if it took the rest of her life. . . ."

"Hattie!" I exclaimed impulsively.

"You are clever, Carolyn. You know, we'd have made a good marriage, you and I. And if it was not for my devotion to completing this task I set for myself years ago, I would have courted you far more intensely than I did. Jeff wouldn't have had a chance."

I said, "Doctor, you must reason this out. You must see how wrong you've been all these years. How many people did you kill? Fourteen? . . ."

"Sixteen. That includes Yvonne. She realized, as you did, that your father's medicine was not meant to cure, but to kill. Always before that I was able to get the bottle before anyone else did, but I failed in this case. Yvonne saw the dead animals, saw the open bottle. I didn't remove either for I was afraid she'd told someone of her suspicions and if that evidence was missing, I'd be suspected. If it was there I could claim that someone had substituted this lethal concoction for the medicine I had prescribed. You know better than to believe that, don't you, Carolyn?"

"Yes," I said. "Have you also killed Jeff and Cal Lindsay?"

"They will not come to your rescue, my dear. Let it go at that. I want to show you something aboard the packet. It may change your mind and make you believe as I did that I was right in what I did. I don't want to hurt you."

"You caused my horse to bolt and I was injured. You fired at me shortly after that. How can I believe you don't wish to harm me?"

"I could have killed you both times. I only wanted to frighten you so that you would go away with your mother. I am in love with you, Carolyn. I know there never has been a chance for me, but that doesn't change the fact that I do love you dearly. That's why I ask that you come with me, so I can show you, aboard the packet—"

"I do not believe you and I never will," I said. "Where is Jeff? What have you done to him?"

"Would it ease your mind if I told you that both he and Cal Lindsay are in hot pursuit of Hattie? Or they think they are. Hattie is long gone from here. I sent her away because I knew this was coming to an end."

"It was you, then, who fired at us when we found the calliope?"

"Of course. And I must say, Jeff succeeded in drawing me away from the carriage. It wasn't until they bumbled about the cabin and the shed where my mother lived that I realized what they were up to, and so I left them and came here in a hurry. Just in time too. As I approached the house, you came out to go down to the rubbish heap. I knew then what you were after and I was finished here."

"You're hurting me," I said. "You don't realize how strong you are."

"I'm sorry." He released me, without thinking, perhaps, because he'd lived the life of a gentleman so long he responded to a woman's request readily. As his hands fell away from my arms, I whirled about and began to run. I took about ten steps before my ankle provided a jolt of pain that swept through my whole body. I couldn't go on. Another step on that ankle and I'd fall.

He was at my side quickly and once again he grasped my arm. "Clever little Carolyn," he said in a changed voice, now cold with anger.

I raised my hands to attack him, to claw at his face, reach his eyes, do anything to get away. He backed me up until I was against the carriage. He held me there while he reached into his coat pocket for a bottle and a piece of cloth. He uncorked the bottle with his teeth, held the cloth to the mouth of the bottle and turned it upside down until the cloth was soaked. I could smell the sweet, pungent odor of chloroform. A doctor would have a supply of that. Suddenly I knew what had happened to Yvonne. Why there were no marks on her body and why it would have been difficult to determine how she died.

The cloth was clapped against my face, but the doctor was in a hurry and careless, for while the cloth was pressed against my face, it was just above my mouth so that I could breathe. The air that went into my lungs was well tainted with chloroform, but had I been breathing through my nose with my mouth closed, I would have been unconscious in seconds.

As it was, I felt my wits spinning. At any second he might realize I was able to draw in some air and remedy that by pressing the cloth against my mouth too. He used his free hand to pour more of the deadly substance onto the cloth, holding me against the carriage with his body. I was too weak to move and he knew it.

In seconds I would succumb to the anesthetic, and if I did, it would be over for me. I let my knees buckle under me and I began to slide down until he seized me. He removed the cloth, held me up, slapped my face half a dozen times until he was satisfied that I was under. He let go of me and I promplty tumbled to the ground. It was not all pretense. I was midway between consciousness and the blackness that came with anesthesia. Evidently he wasn't going to kill me with the chloroform, perhaps because it would have been too obvious. He had other plans for me.

I remained limp when he picked me up and deposited me on the seat of the carriage. He clambered aboard himself and the horse obeyed the crack of the whip by moving away very quickly.

I felt myself slipping off the seat. There was a chance I might fall out of the carriage, but I had to risk it and I let myself slide down like someone utterly helpless and completely under the influence of the anesthetic.

Dr. Shea seized my arm and hauled me back onto the seat without slowing up the horse. I didn't know where we were going. I didn't dare to even partly open my eyes for fear he'd notice. I was dealing with a doctor who knew all about the effects of this drug. My life hung in the balance and I had to be most careful.

I could wait for an opportunity to escape, though I wondered how I'd ever get away from him, for I was weak. I doubted my limbs would respond if I tried to run. The chloroform hadn't quite rendered me unconscious, but so close to it that I was still affected and likely would be for some time.

I didn't have much hope of rescue. Jeff and Cal were likely searching for Hattie in the belief that it had been she who'd fired at us. Jeff would think me safe in the house, armed with guns and warned to use them if necessary.

I must have succumbed to the effects of the anesthetic for a time because I seemed to be unaware of anything until I felt myself being carried. There was a certain springiness to Dr. Shea's steps as he moved and I quickly realized that he was carrying me across the gangplank to the packet.

My mind cleared promptly, since I had not been inhaling the chloroform for several minutes now, but I remained limp as if deep in unconsciousness.

It was dark, which slowed him a great deal and gave me a slight amount of hope for time that might work in my favor. I had only Jeff and Cal Lindsay to depend upon. I knew it was a forlorn hope that they'd reach me in time, but I refused to give up. At the first opportunity I meant to attempt to escape again. I would take full advantage of the slightest lapse in Dr. Shea's vigilance.

All of which proved to me, quite painfully, that I was too much the optimist. Before I knew it he had placed me on deck, knelt and began tying my hands behind my back. I struggled, because there'd never be another chance and he laughed at my efforts.

"So you weren't under all the time. I took your pulse more than once and I felt quite sure you were shamming. It makes no difference. I promise you this. Whatever happens, I'll make it easy for you."

"What will you gain by killing me?" I asked. "You're going to be caught."

"No, I won't be. Mother and I have everything all arranged. We're sailing for Europe early Tuesday morning. From New Orleans. We'll be well away from here before anyone suspects me."

"What will you do with me?"

"As I said, I'll make it easy for you. As I did for poor Yvonne. Just as you did, she saw the dead animals and suspected the medicine. I caught her coming back from the refuse heap and she gave her suspicions away by trying to run. I put her to sleep and carried her back to the path, where I arranged the body so it would look as if she'd suffered a heart seizure. That was what I intended to offer as cause of death if it became necessary."

He had, by now, succeeded in tying my ankles. He picked me up again and carried me all the way to the hurricane deck.

"I wish I could have arranged to have the calliope here so I might imitate the ship's whistle with it. The whistle and the bell were an inspiration. My mother thought of that. You know, she used to travel on the packet with papa and she played the calliope. She was very good at it. After the ship ran aground and partly burned, she had the calliope removed. I helped her repaint it and repair the damage from the fire. Mama is very clever."

"She is mad," I said. "She has turned you to madness as well. You were only a young man when the packet ran aground. You wouldn't have kept all this hate locked up in your heart if she had not influenced you so strongly over the years."

"Be careful," he said in a cold warning. "I love my mother and anyone who speaks against her answers to me. I could make this extremely hard for you, my dear Carolyn. Don't bring that upon yourself."

He straightened up and left me on the deck. I didn't know where he went, but presently I detected the smell of oil. Then I heard him moving around on the lower deck. When he returned to the upper deck, he sloshed more oil over the bleached, aged wood. I knew then that he was going to make a funeral pyre of this ship and I was to be burned to death.

I raised my head and uttered a piercing scream. I cried out again and again until he slapped his hand over my mouth.

"If you do that again I'll not use chloroform on you, but let you feel the agony of the flames. Don't underestimate me, Carolyn. I may be in love with you, but I'm more bent on avenging my father's death. Your father could have given orders to save people on this packet, but he refused. That's why he died, and that's why you will also die. I'm only sorry I can't kill the rest of them, the mindless people who stood by and watched others die that night."

"Doctor," I said, "you are not in your right mind. Consider what you are doing. This will only result in your death too. You cannot get away with it. They'll know you are responsible for my being burned. They'll hunt you down if it takes years."

"Let them hunt. I told you, mama and I have everything ready so we'll disappear from the face of the earth. No one can possibly find us. We've had years to plan it and it's foolproof. I'm sorry, Carolyn, but I can't delay any longer. To meet mama and make that boat I can't afford to waste any more time. I only hope that, somehow, your father knows what's going on and that he is in some way able to know how it feels to have someone he loves being burned to death."

He arose to his full height and opened the bottle of

chloroform again. He soaked the cloth. "As I said, I can't stand you being in agony, so I'll put you to sleep . . . ."

I yelled. As loudly as I could. I thrashed about, rolling across the deck. He had placed me close to the stairs leading to the deck below and somehow I managed to roll right on down those steps before he could stop me.

He gave a wild yell of rage and started after me. I fell all the way down, somehow managing not to injure myself so that I'd become unconscious. I landed on my back and I could see Dr. Shea at the top of the narrow stairway. He seemed to be frozen there for a few seconds. I heard the sound of a shot. This time Dr. Shea tumbled backwards and landed on the deck with his legs hanging over the edge of the stairs. I thought that Dr. Shea must have been hit while I was on my way down and he'd been standing there, a perfect target, frozen in pain, or perhaps near death, so that the marksman was able to fire again with deadly accuracy.

Those things went through my mind as I gradually felt myself sinking into the unconsciousness I'd so far avoided. I didn't fight it. I was only too glad to escape into that void of darkness.

"She's waking up," someone said. "Carolyn, it's all right now. You're safe. Wake up, darling! Please wake up."

I managed to open my eyes. I was in the carriage, my head resting on Jeff's lap. I tried to speak, but I found it impossible, partly because Jeff bent and kissed me. I was content then. I closed my eyes once more.

Someone was forcing brandy between my lips. I gagged slightly, but the potent liquor did help. I was able to sit up after a little while. I was in the drawing room of my own home. Jeff sat beside the sofa on which I lay. Cal Lindsay, holding the decanter of brandy and a glass, smiled at me, poured a generous portion of brandy and downed it himself. I didn't blame him.

In a short time I was myself again, shaken, but able to face up to the memory of what had almost happened to me.

Cal said, "It was too close. By the time Jeff and I decided we weren't leading anybody away from you, it was too late. I don't think Hattie was even around. It must have been Shea."

"It was," I said. "He told me enough so I know all of the answers now. Or most of them."

"Do you feel up to telling us?" Jeff asked. "We found evidence in Hattie's cabin that she must have been Shea's mother."

"She was. I. . . ." Suddenly I remembered those last few seconds. "Where is Dr. Shea? I fell down the stairs . . . or whatever you call them. . . ."

"Ladder," Jeff said with a smile.

"All right. Anyway, when I hit the bottom, Dr. Shea was standing on the top deck, holding onto the rails as if he was about to come charging down to me. But he didn't move. He just stood there and then there was a shot. . . ."

"Yes, we know. The first bullet must have stunned him, but he didn't fall. The second one put him down."

"He is dead?" I asked.

"Dead," Call said curtly.

"Then I have you two to thank. . . ."

"Not us," Jeff said. "It was Willie Spencer who killed him. Willie had gone to Hattie's cabin and removed the rifle, luckily, so he was armed when he needed the use of a gun. He was watching the packet, thinking that something was due to happen. He didn't see Shea carry you aboard, but he heard you scream. He had to wait until he had a good target. When he did, he fired."

"Willie is a pretty good shot," Cal commented.

I said, "Hattie is on her way to New Orleans where she was to wait for Dr. Shea. They were taking a ship to some foreign land where they could hide, or whatever they intended to do."

"What caused him to try and kill you?" Jeff asked.

"I discovered that he gradually poisoned his victims, caused them to sicken and slowly die. When he was ready, he provided a deadly dose of his so-called medicine. Hattie would be told about when the next victim would die, and she'd bring the calliope down to the far side of the packet. It likely had steam up already and she simply played that note which sounded like the ship's whistle. She rang the bell and then brought everything back to her place. The calliope had to be kept hidden. That's why she'd permitted no one to come near her place and she was ready to use the rifle if anyone insisted."

"Shea was responsible for the first two attempts on your life?" Jeff asked. "I mean the slingshot used on your horse and the shot fired at you?"

"He said he only wanted to scare me away from the plantation," I said.

"That was kind of him," Cal observed caustically.

"Did he brag about setting the cane fields afire?" Jeff asked. "And do you know where Ed Baker is?"

"At Dr. Shea's office. I don't know how Ed Baker got into the fields."

"I can guess," Cal said. "He got drunk on bad booze. He went to the Austin house and tried to get in. Randy beat him up and I think Ed must have gone blind from that beating. Maybe it was the booze. Who knows? But I think Ed wandered around and got into the cane field by accident. He fell asleep. When he woke up and found he couldn't see he started yelling. You heard him. Shea must have been close by and he heard him too. When you went after him, Shea took advantage of the situation by setting the fields on fire. That's only a theory, but I'll bet it will hold up."

"I think so too," I said. "In a way I feel sorry for Dr. Shea. I believe his mother filled him so full of the poison of hatred and a desire for revenge that he too was not completely responsible."

"That doesn't change the fact that he killed many people," Cal said. "We should have suspected him. Nobody died until after he arrived here. His mother had to bide her time until he grew up and got out of medical school. By the time that happened, she was ready."

"How do you feel now?" Jeff asked.

"I'm all right, I think."

"Can you stand a carriage ride down to the packet?"

"The old ship? Why, Jeff?"

"I want you to be a witness to the last rites. Shea got her all ready for burning and we're going to finish the job. His body was removed some time ago, while you were sleeping. We saved the last act until you were able to witness it."

"Take me there," I said. "When that packet is destroyed, then we can be sure Captain Haley's mad curse is destroyed too. I wouldn't want to miss that."

Jeff and I sat in the carriage, looking up at the hulk while Cal went aboard and set it afire. He came over the gangplank at a dead run with the flames not too far behind him. The weathered old wood burned like tinder. It was almost dawn as the fire lit up the sky, and by the time the sun rose, there was little left. A few twisted bits of metal, heaps of ash and some smoke, idly curling up into the sky.

Jeff turned the carriage about, waited until Cal got aboard and drove us back to the house.

The villagers soon returned. Once made aware of what had really happened, they were glad to return. The village quickly grew more prosperous than ever. Jeff and I were married soon after all the excitement died down. We've lived in the plantation house ever since. Mama comes to visit and when we start our family she will probably come to stay, but at the moment she refuses to remain more than a day or two. There are too many dark memories lingering here to suit her nervous nature.

Ed Baker died a few weeks after we had destroyed the old packet. Willie Spencer still lives in his cabin, happily and quietly. I owe him my life, so that I see he comes to supper often and it is my only regret that he desires nothing, wants for nothing, so there are few ways I can repay him.

Cal stayed on. With the authority of a partner in the plantation, he now supervises all the help he needs. The new cane grew well on the burned-out fields and the dock at the river is now busier than when papa lived.

Randy Austin came back to run his plantation and to boast that he would soon be so successful he'd buy ours. It turned out to be the other way around. Randy quickly found difficulties he could not overcome, and finally Jeff and I bought his place and he went off to New Orleans. We never heard of him since.

Jeff and I are supremely happy. He gave up his New Orleans office and devotes all his time to raising sugar cane. Sometimes I find myself associating the mansion with the evil things that had happened to me, but then I tell myself I'd be foolish to let this affect my life and Jeff's. It will all pass in time, I know. Papa would have been proud of what Jeff and I have done with the foundation he laid down, and that makes me content and happy.

The knoll where the packet had rested so many years has been cleared of the debris and it is now grass covered, with nothing left to remind anyone of the tragedy which had turned into a nightmare.

"EVEN IF YOU HAVEN'T EXERCISED ONCE IN THE LAST TWENTY YEARS, YOU ARE JUST TWO HOURS* AWAY FROM GOOD PHYSICAL CONDITION."

*(These hours represent the cumulative time of 30 minutes-a-week program.)

"Even if you haven't exercised once in the last twenty years, you are just two hours* away from good physical condition ...and at the end of twelve hours,* you'll be in excellent shape by any standards."

T❁TAL FITNESS IN 30 MINUTES A WEEK

LAURENCE E. MOREHOUSE, PH.D.
PROFESSOR OF EXERCISE PHYSIOLOGY AND DIRECTOR OF THE HUMAN PERFORMANCE LABORATORY, UNIVERSITY OF CALIFORNIA AT LOS ANGELES
AND LEONARD GROSS

These hours represent the cumulative time of a 30-minute-a-week program

Total Fitness in 30 Minutes A Week may be the most stimulating and effective physical-fitness plan ever published. Dr. Morehouse not only shows you what real fitness is ("fit for what?"), but how to achieve it at any age once and for all, and how you can easily and quickly acquire a reserve of physical well-being that will make you look younger, feel better, and probably live longer by exercising his way for only thirty minutes a week.

Two weeks after starting the Total Fitness plan you will find a startling change in yourself—a new energy, a new vitality, a youthful buoyancy that will amaze you.

SEND FOR YOUR FREE EXAMINATION COPY OF TOTAL FITNESS IN 30 MINUTES A WEEK TODAY.

You need send no money. Just mail the coupon to Simon and Schuster, Dept. F-10, 630 Fifth Avenue, New York, N.Y. 10020. ▼

SIMON & SCHUSTER, INC., Dept. F-10
630 Fifth Avenue • New York, N.Y. 10020

Please send me a copy of *Total Fitness In 30 Minutes A Week* for a free, two-week examination. If I am not convinced that it can make me look, feel and act younger and healthier, I will return it and owe nothing. Otherwise, I will send $6.95, plus mailing costs, as payment in full.

NAME_____

ADDRESS_____

CITY_____STATE_____ZIP_____

☐ SAVE POSTAGE. Check here if you enclose $6.95 as payment in full. We will pay all mailing costs. Same two-week return privilege with full refund guaranteed.

x 7/1

How to stay healthy all the time.

> "I can recommend this book for authoritative answers to questions that continually come up about health and how to live."—Harry J. Johnson, M.D., Chairman, Medical Board Director, Life Extension Institute.

Wouldn't it be wonderful if your whole family could stay healthy all the time?

It may now be possible, thanks to PREVENTIVE MEDICINE. This is the modern approach to health care. Its goal is to prevent illness before it even has a chance to strike!

A new book called THE FAMILY BOOK OF PREVENTIVE MEDICINE shows how you can take advantage of this preventive approach, and make it an everyday reality for yourself and your family. More than 700 pages long—and written in clear, simple language.

TELLS YOU ALL ABOUT THE LATEST MEDICAL ADVANCES

For example, the new knowledge of risk factors in disease is a vital tool of preventive medicine. With it, your doctor might pinpoint you as, say, a high heart attack risk *long before* your *heart actually gives you any trouble*. He could then prescribe certain changes in your diet and habits—perhaps very minor ones—that could remove the danger entirely. This would be preventive medicine at its ideal best! But even if a disease has already taken root, new diagnostic techniques can reveal its presence earlier than ever before. And, as a rule, the sooner a disease is discovered, the more easily it is cured.

SEND NO MONEY—10 DAYS' FREE EXAMINATION

Mail the coupon below, and THE FAMILY BOOK OF PREVENTIVE MEDICINE will be sent to you for free examination. Then, if you are not convinced that it can help you protect the health of your entire family, return it within 10 days and owe nothing. Otherwise, we will bill you for $12.95 plus mailing costs. At all bookstores, or write to Simon and Schuster, Dept. S-53, 630 Fifth Ave., New York, N.Y. 10020.